Confessions of a Saleswoman

Confessions of a Saleswoman

Anatomy of the Game

Teasing Tom

Exposure at the Tradeshow

My Meeting with Robert, College Memories,
and a Gift to My Husband

SARA SHAE BOWMAN

DISCLAIMER

Confessions of a Saleswoman may contain content that some readers may find offensive or disturbing. This disclaimer is intended to notify readers in advance about the nature of the content within the book. This book may include but is not limited to explicit language, graphic sexual content, sexually sensitive topics, or sexual themes including but not limited to multiple partners, same-sex, extra-marital affairs, exhibitionism, coercion, and masochism.

Readers are advised that the content may not be suitable for all audiences and reader discretion is advised.

By choosing to read *Confessions of a Saleswoman*, readers acknowledge and accept the presence of potentially offensive content within the book.

This is a work of fiction. Unless otherwise indicated, all the names, characters, businesses, places, events and incidents in this book are either the product of the author's imagination or used in a fictitious manner. Any resemblance to actual persons, living or dead, or actual events is purely coincidental. All characters represented in this work are of legal age of consent.

ISBN: 979-8-9929784-2-1

First Edition: April 2025

"For me at least, when I feel sexy, I feel confident, and wearing a garter belt and stockings with four-inch heels and barely-there panties under a thin flowing dress definitely feels sexy."

~ Anonymous Saleswoman

Contents

Prologue: Anatomy of the Game

Confession One: Teasing Tom

 Contents (cont.)

Confession Two: Exposure at the Tradeshow

Contents *(cont.)*

Confession Three: My Meeting with Robert, College Memories, and a Gift to My Husband

Prologue:

Anatomy of the Game

The Tease

Remember sitting in front of the Christmas tree, looking at the presents that you weren't allowed to open? Because you wanted any hint you could possibly get to what's inside, you were drawn to the little things, trying to find that opening.

You would look at the ribbon on top, seeing the ends of the bow, knowing just a slight tug would untie it. You would notice a slight tear in the paper, wondering if it could be opened a little more—accidentally of course! You might see how the overlap in the wrapping is puckered up slightly—maybe you could see through the gap. You might even run your fingers over the surfaces, careful not to arouse any suspicion, feeling for any ridges or indications of what may, or may not, be underneath.

And given enough time, enough building anticipation, your curiosity and overconfidence will get the best of you. If you think no one will see you—and no one will stop you— you will try to unwrap it slightly to reveal the prize.

You didn't know it then, but as an adult you realize your parents knew exactly what you did. It was just a matter of whether they were amused by your actions, or wanted to scold you and make you stop.

I learned a long time ago, that is exactly how the interaction plays out when an attractive, professionally dressed woman walks into a man's office for a meeting or sales call. Nine times out of ten, I know, or at least get a strong indication, of his thoughts the second I meet a male client. His body language, his smile, the tone in his voice, the way he touches me when he greets me, and the visual peruse of my body that he's not even aware he does.

Most women can read these signs, especially more mature or experienced women. Some pick up on only the obvious, while others see every little nuance as flashing neon. It is an art and a skill.

Many women respond by becoming cold or overly professional, some feel threatened, some offended. Pantsuits,

4

long skirts, flats and baggy tops are usually the attire of these women. Some other women feel flattered, complemented, attractive, even desired, but they will never let that show. They are either too career driven, faithfully married, or too nervous or scared to embrace it. Some of them are even naive to what they wear and the effect it has on a man, whether that was their intent or not.

And then the smallest group. The group I proudly claim. The women who embrace the game, the flirting, the teasing, the subtle brush of a hand or trace of a finger. The women who fuel the fantasies of every straight man, denying it to their wives, then taking matters into their own hands when left alone with their deviant thoughts. I love being that woman. It makes me feel alive. It intoxicates and arouses me. I would even say it's become an addiction.

There's such a feeling of power, knowing a man looks at you with desire, knowing he'll remember you, and think of you after you leave. No doubt letting his imagination put you in all sorts of compromising positions on, and under, his desk.

The Wrapping

When I'm preparing for a meeting, whether it's a new client or one I've met several times before, I painstakingly go over every detail, every nuance, even the smallest.

I'm not talking about my sales contract or product pitch—no, I have all that down. I'm talking about every nuance of what I'm going to wear, how I'm going to greet him, how and where I'm going to sit, how I plan to tease, and even how far I plan to go.

My body is the present, and the clothing is the wrapping. First, I'll take note of where every button falls, every zipper, and every tie. I look at where the material gaps between buttons, perhaps revealing the undercurve of my breast. How the wrap of a skirt opens when I walk or falls off my leg when I sit. Is it enough to hide the tops of my stockings or will I need to wear sheer pantyhose.

Which zippers like to work themselves down as I move, or which snaps will come undone when I turn too far in a particular way. A perfectly timed wardrobe malfunction is always an innocent way to tease.

How does the material of a particular dress lie against my body? Does it reveal the lines of my panties, or garter straps? Can I get away without a bra, and do my nipples show if I'm aroused? I hope so.

How sheer is the material? Perhaps my body is silhouetted through a flowing dress when I walk in front of a window or can the lace pattern on the cups of my bra be made out.

And don't even get me started on my shoes! Finding the perfect pair of heels, paired with the right hosiery, can take the outfit to another level. Pumps, slingbacks, peep-toes, D'orsay—so many choices, but all with no less than a four-inch heel. I've used a pesky buckle on an ankle strap on more than one occasion to allow a handsome man the opportunity to touch my nylon clad legs or give just the right angle to see my hidden secrets when I ask him for his help securing it.

Although I will go with bare legs most of the summer, or with a trend, I do have a special affection for hosiery. Ever since wearing my first pair of tights in grade school, discovering pantyhose as a teen, and then thigh-highs and stockings later in college, there's just something about feeling them on my legs that makes me feel sexy. In my personal experience, the right style, pattern, or texture on your legs can act as an irresistible magnet to most men's eyes—and hands.

It's no secret that men are visual creatures, and just by watching their eyes, I can usually learn what turns them on within a few seconds.

The Men

Once I've put together the perfect outfit, professional yet provocative, paired with just the right high heels, and barely concealing my lingerie, or lack thereof, it's time to visit my client. My approach may be different depending on the visit. Some clients are in an industrial setting, others in high rises, and a few may be in a home office.

In the case of an existing client, I'm adjusting my wardrobe, demeanor, and expected level of personal interaction based on my experience with them. I try to learn what turns them on, what they can't resist, what I need to be for them. Are they a leg man, or do they prefer breasts? Am I wearing that skirt with the high slit up the middle of the front, or that nearly sheer blouse unbuttoned to the middle of my breasts?

Do they like a woman who is assertive, in charge, aggressive, or do they prefer to be the dominant one, making me feel submissive as they stand over me, trembling at their touch.

Maybe they clearly have lines they won't let themselves cross but enjoy seeing every inch of my body that I dare reveal. Content with the view down my blouse, hanging open as I lean over their desk, or the unobstructed view between my thighs, exposing my panties, or more, as I sit pretending to be distracted with my legs parting in their direction.

Most men fit the category of the voyeur, taking their chances, hoping to catch a glimpse of something they weren't meant to see. These are the fun men, because they are typically the gentleman, not wanting to offend or be "that guy", but still no less horny inside. These are the men that "the game" is truly played with, flirting back and forth, building trust and a level of comfort.

Most of them have the desire inside of them. Given the right encouragement and insurance that no one will ever know, they will truly appreciate and welcome it if I were to lower myself to my knees in front of them, or bend over their desk and look back, telling them, "Take me however you want."

The smallest group of men, the ones I honestly see very rarely, are those who are all about the business. They are either closet gay, madly in love with their wives, having some other issue that's completely killing their sex drive, or too paranoid that they're going to get sued for sexual harassment to do anything inappropriate.

Although not the typical type of fun I have in a meeting, it can also be entertaining trying to break their shell. I might say something inappropriate or go through an entire meeting with a short skirt hiked up enough to remove any doubt that I'm not wearing panties under my hose.

The third group of men are the ones I must be on the defensive with when playing "the game". They are the men that greet you with a hug and call you honey or look at your cleavage and back up to your eyes with a grin and a wink. They will tell you a dirty joke and then reach over and squeeze your thigh as they laugh at it. And it's completely possible they will place their hand on your rear as you stand beside their desk.

It's not that I'm not going to use all my tricks and charm and "assets", it's that I have to do it in a really controlled way and have a clear idea of how far I'm going to let them go. In their mind, from the moment we met, they were planning how to get me to a hotel room.

While repeat visits to existing clients are enjoyable in their own way, depending on the relationship that's been built, there are now expectations and a level of comfort. That's why I still get so excited when I meet a new client. It's the unknown, like a blind date. The excitement and nervousness as you learn their personality and try to identify their erotic triggers. He is still a stranger, so it can be incredibly arousing the first times I expose myself, revealing an intimate part of my body, watching for his reaction.

Does he look uncomfortable or excited? Does he lean a certain way or shift in his seat? Does he lick his lips or swallow, or maybe adjust his collar? But most importantly, does he look again?

Who Am I?

Up to this point, you might be picturing me walking into an office, dressed like a slut, sitting with my legs spread, trading sex for a signed purchase order, regardless of the man I'm meeting. Sounds like the plot of a low budget adult movie.

I do try to hold myself to a higher standard than that, and like to think the men I'm meeting—at least most of them—are a little more sophisticated.

I'm not a single, low self-esteem, cheap floozy. I'm actually a wife, a loving mother, and a confident driven professional, like so many women. But I also like sex. Some men may be surprised to hear it, but yes, women like sex too. We just have always been told we have to keep that a secret or get labeled a slut.

Whether I'm wearing a leather bustier with a garter belt, or sheer pantyhose and a lace bra, or naked with only high heels and thigh-highs under my dress at work, from all outward appearances, I will look professional and classy until I decide to reveal what's underneath.

Do I enjoy teasing, flashing, and flirting? Absolutely, every chance I get. But that doesn't mean I do it with every man I meet. Let's be honest, looks do matter—to an extent. However, the first thing that turns me on or off is his personality. If I meet an attractive man, and he is mean, or just a jerk, then I will be pleasant and professional. But my blouse will stay buttoned, and my legs will stay crossed. On the other hand, if I meet a man who, for whatever reason, just isn't that physically attractive, but clearly has a heart of gold, a sense of humor, and generally a good person, then I'm going to feel comfortable flirting. And I will be a lot more likely to want to give him a little tease or something special, because I feel he deserves it.

Am I having sex, or dropping to my knees with all my clients? Of course not! I do still have a professional reputation, and family and friends, so when a situation does get physical, it's either with a stranger, someone out of town, or someone who has just as much risk as I do.

Regardless of how hot he is, if he's single and close to home, I'm not going to make myself vulnerable to rumors since he has nothing to lose.

If I met with a hundred clients, twenty-five of them would be a typical boring sales meeting. Seventy meetings would have some level of flirting, teasing, flashing, or maybe even light touching. Depending on the setting, a hand on my leg is not that uncommon. I've attended many dinner meetings or cocktail hours going over a sales contract on top of the table while a hand explores my thigh under the table. I've even had the occasional roaming hand cup my breast or bottom after a few too many drinks at cocktail hour.

Five of the meetings might turn into the office door locked and me surrendering myself to their fantasies. But for this to happen, there had to be chemistry, attraction, and a sense of safety for both of us that it would be kept between us.

I'm not having ongoing affairs with any of these men. There is no emotional attachment, just erotic encounters. Most are one-time things. Only a few have happened more than once but spread out over time.

Why do I do it? Am I not happy at home—not getting fulfilled? Every married couple knows the ups and downs of life together, even if things are good, it still gets a little mundane. You can play little games and have date nights trying to recapture what you had when you dated, but it's different after twenty-some years.

These experiences are exciting—plain and simple. They are new, uncertain, exhilarating, even risky. No matter how many times over the years I've told myself, "I really should stop— this is the last time," I find myself sitting across the desk from some handsome older man, seeing his eyes drop to my legs where my hemline has ridden up, and I feel the warm tingle.

After years of playing this game, I've stopped trying to fight it and embraced it—embracing that I'm a woman who loves sex.

What Have I Become?

While everything I've described about the nuances of "The Game" that I play has held true and steady throughout the years, one thing has evolved—me. The nuances of clothing, body language, teasing, and flirting that can be so arousing and intoxicating during an interaction remain the same, but my tolerances and limits have been tested and pushed. Over the years, and after many flings, desires and fantasies have been awakened, and I've been exposed to so many more kinks and turn-ons that I never even realized aroused me so greatly.

The way an adrenaline junkie needs to always go faster, higher, or harder to get the same thrill—I too have let myself surrender at times, finding myself caught up in the moment.

This was probably never truer than when I attended the trade show and met Aaron—but I don't want to get ahead of myself.

I know what you're thinking—enough with all the underlying details, analyzing, and self-reflection—confess already! So, confess I will—every naughty detail.

I'm going to share the stories of Tom, Aaron, and Robert— three of the more memorable encounters I've had over the years. I've never shared any of this with anyone before, so please keep it between us.

Let me start with Tom.

Confession One:

Teasing Tom

CHAPTER ONE

Sally's Garage

Tom was not the most attractive, or the biggest account, or the craziest sex. Tom was sweet and sincere, and I loved what I was able to be for him.

As I usually do with new client meetings whenever possible, I scheduled my first on-site with Tom at three in the afternoon. This lets the appointment be open-ended for me. If things get interesting or a plan is made to go to happy hour, it works out. If it's a bust or wraps quickly, I get to head home early.

In case you're wondering what it is that I do, I work in the glamorous world of paper clips, copiers, and everything it takes to keep the workplace running. I try to get clients under contract and then we handle all their equipment leasing and supply needs. I know it's not the most exciting business, but for me it's more about the people I get to meet. The money is not too bad either, especially if I get a large contract and earn commissions.

Tom and his wife owned a small local chain of auto repair shops called *Sally's Garage*, after his wife I presume. After speaking with him on the phone and getting a feel for his needs, we set up an appointment to discuss some of the details and finalize the equipment. I remember being struck by how soft spoken and kind he sounded.

It was a beautiful spring day, not too hot yet, with a light breeze. I was wearing a short sleeve, cream-colored wrap dress that tied at the hips. It fell a few inches above my knees, and I intentionally left the ties a little loose, letting the layers fall more freely across my body as I moved. My cream-colored, slingback high heels clicked on the concrete as I walked past the two open garage bay doors, getting the attention of the three men working in the garage. I glanced over at them and smiled as I felt their eyes moving over my body with every step.

Once inside the front office, the young lady working at the counter told me Tom was finishing up a call and would be right out, so I had a seat in the small waiting room. There was only one other person waiting there, a man in a gray suit, looking to be in his thirties, scrolling on his phone.

When I sat down, he looked up and we exchanged acknowledging smiles, followed by the subconscious drop of his eyes to my legs as I crossed them in his direction. I smiled to myself as I knew he had just caught a glimpse of the lace band at the top of my sheer nude stay-up thigh-highs, revealed on the underside of my crossed leg where my dress was hanging freely. He pretended to look back at his phone, but he was really enjoying the view I was providing.

After a few minutes, Tom appeared from the back and apologized for keeping me waiting as he led me to his office. He was not quite what I expected him to look like, being the owner of a garage. Somehow, I was picturing a gruffer appearance, maybe a beard and jeans with a button-up work shirt. He appeared to be in his fifties, short hair with a touch of salt and pepper, clean shaven, wearing a tan polo shirt with a dark pair of khakis. I also couldn't help noticing the smell of his cologne; it was subtle but very intoxicating. The beautiful gold watch adorning his muscular forearms also stood out to me, both admittedly a turn on of mine.

He greeted me, politely shook my hand, and I couldn't help but notice how large and powerful his hands were as they completely enveloped mine. When he led me into his office, I felt his hand lightly brush across my lower back as he pulled a chair out in front of his desk.

Just like my impression on the phone, he seemed very kind and had a manner about him that made me feel at ease. Rather than sit behind his desk, he pulled another chair up beside me. Before getting down to business, we talked for quite some time. He was very charming, and very easy to talk to. There was a level of comfort between us immediately that seemed a little easier than normal.

He opened up and shared how he and his wife had built their business from the ground up, but I was surprised to learn that his wife unexpectedly passed away almost a year earlier. I could tell he was feeling emotional and missed her, especially when he shared with me that I reminded him of her in my appearance. He even used the words "uncanny resemblance".

I noticed repeatedly through our conversation, his eyes would drop down to my legs as I sat, turned toward him, with them crossed in his direction. It would even appear as if he got lost for a few seconds, just staring at my high heel, and then slowly moving up my shin and over my knee to where the top layer of my dress lay over my thigh.

We eventually turned our attention to business. After a few minutes of me droning on about different details, I took out the paperwork and laid it on the front of his desk. I hadn't even planned it, but when I slid forward in my seat to lay the papers out, it pulled just enough on the top wrap of my dress to make it fall off my thigh. Exposed was the entire lace band at the top of my nylons and an inch or so of bare skin above it.

I honestly didn't even notice it at first as I arranged the papers and started pointing out different line items. After a moment, I could tell he was distracted and that's when I realized how I was exposed. It was really nothing that bad, but still sexy and erotic visually. I acted embarrassed—slightly more than I actually was—apologizing as I started to pull my dress back over my leg. I looked up at him, smiling, to see his reaction and it was not at all what I expected.

He was crying.

What? Why is he crying? Oh my God …

I looked at him and asked with compassion, "What's wrong? Are you okay?"

Instinctively, I reached out and put my hand on his leg, in a caring gesture. I'll admit, I have seen a lot of reactions over the years to flashing a man, but crying has never been one of them! I could tell he was embarrassed as he wiped the tears away and cleared his throat. Again, I consoled him, "It's okay—you can tell me—what's wrong? Did I say something to upset you?"

His voice cracked as he responded, "It's nothing, really, I can't—it's not appropriate for me to say. You just … You just remind me of my wife that's all—I'm sorry."

I assured him sincerely, as I gently rubbed his thigh, saying, "It's okay, you can tell me. I insist—I want to know—you're not going to offend me, I swear."

"Are you sure?"

"Yes, absolutely, please, I want to know."

He took a deep breath and composed himself before saying, "It was when your dress fell off your leg, seeing the lace at the top of the nylons you're wearing."

"I'm sorry, did I offend you somehow, I didn't—"

He interrupted me, putting his large hand down over mine and squeezing it, saying, "No, no ... Heavens no—quite the opposite—it was a beautiful thing."

"It's just that my wife would wear stockings and garter belts all the time for me. She knew how much I appreciated them on a woman. It's just always been my thing. And it was something we would do, when she was feeling playful, or teasing me. She would sit across from me and uncross her legs or slide her dress up to show me her stockings ... or more, sometimes even in public."

Pausing for only a second to take a deep breath, he continued, "So, when your dress fell open, and I saw your stockings, those memories crashed back, and I felt how much I missed that—I'm sorry, it's embarrassing, and I ... I shouldn't be telling you this."

I felt so bad for him as I reached over and put my other hand on top of his, I assured him, "Please don't feel embarrassed—that's a beautiful memory—I completely understand."

We sat there quietly, smiling at each other, sharing that moment. He broke the silence, trying to pull things back to our business meeting, clearly still embarrassed that he shared with me.

"Okay, so go over these lines again here," he said in his best professional tone.

I paused for a few seconds, looking at him, smiling, when I decided I wanted to try to give him something more. I just looked at him with a subtle smile as he watched me bring my hand back over to my leg where I pinched the material of the hem between my thumb and forefinger and slowly pulled it back off my leg, all the way up to my hip. I brought my hand back up to the desk where I picked up the pen, now sitting with my entire thigh exposed for him.

He smiled back at me, clearly feeling emotional again, he said, "Thank you. But you really don't have to do that."

I smiled again and simply replied, "You're quite welcome—and I know I don't have to, but I want to. It's nice to feel appreciated by a handsome man."

During the rest of the meeting, his attention was clearly split between my legs and my paperwork, but we got through it. Once we finished, there were some changes that needed to be made, and I told him I would come by the next day with a copy for him to sign. recalling the details

Business aside now, we stood up and again he thanked me for my understanding. I told him it was my pleasure, and I initiated giving him a hug. At first, he was a little tense when he put his arms around my back, but when I held on to him, hugging him in a consoling way, I felt his arms relax, squeezing in a more tender way as his hands moved softly over my back. I made no effort to pull away, letting him hold me there as long as he wanted.

I could feel one of his hands dropping lower and lower down my back until it rested at the very top of my butt. I could almost sense that he wanted so badly to drop his hand down and caress me but was fighting back the urge. His hands finally both dropped down to the outside of my hips as he pushed my body back, smiling and saying, "Thank you again—you don't know how much that meant to me."

Once more, I assured him it was my pleasure, as I gathered my things, and he walked me all the way out to my car. He opened the door for me like a gentleman, and doing my part to not disappoint, I let my dress fall open as I slid into my seat.

I told him I would be back around the same time tomorrow with the papers to sign, and I would be happy to stay for a little while and talk some more if he would like. He smiled and said, "That would be nice, thank you."

Shutting the door to my car, he stood for a moment looking in through the window. I smiled at him, gave a little wink, and casually flipped the other side of the wrap at the bottom of my dress off my leg, now letting him see both of my thighs all the way to the top of my nylons. He just smiled and gave a little shake of his head as I drove off.

CHAPTER TWO

A Special Day For Tom

That evening, I went up to my closet to pick out what I was going to wear the next day. Playing back the conversation with Tom in my mind and recalling the details he shared, I decided right then I wanted to wear something special for him—something I knew he would truly love.

I pulled everything out of my closet for my outfit and laid it neatly on the chair in the corner. My husband would already be gone to work in the morning when I got dressed so he wouldn't be questioning what I was wearing.

The next morning after my bath, I patted my body dry with a soft towel, my skin feeling extra sensitive everywhere I just smoothly shaved. With my hair and makeup finished, I walked into my bedroom naked.

First, picking up the dainty pink and cream-colored garter belt, I slid it around my waist and clipped it, spinning it into position. Next, I slid my sheer nude nylons up my legs, smoothing them around my thighs, and then carefully clipping them to the garter straps.

I pulled the matching G-string panty up around my hips, over top of the garter belt, feeling the thin string of material slip up against my most intimate areas between my cheeks. The small triangle of sheer pink material barely formed over my freshly shaved lips, covering me but still revealing the tender slit that was underneath.

I slipped my arms through the straps of the bra and wrapped it around to clip the front closure at the center of my breasts. Similar to the G-string panty, the bra had cream lace accents, but the cups were a sheer pink nylon that did nothing to hide my nipples. One at a time, I lowered my stocking covered feet into a pair of cream-colored, D'orsay cut, four-inch-high heels.

Finally, I put on my dress. A short sleeve, button-up dress with a hem that fell just below my knees. There were several large buttons down the front, but I only left one open at the top and bottom. I wanted to look classy, proper, and conservative at first.

I love the feeling when I first get dressed in an outfit like this. It feels so sexy, the light material of the dress moving over my body yet feeling the intimate apparel I'm wearing underneath against my skin. I know I'm completely covered but can't help feeling like everyone I walk past knows what I'm wearing underneath.

When I got to work, I quickly fell into my routine, and before I knew it was time to leave to go meet Tom. I parked around the side of his building, made a last check of my hair and lipstick in the rear-view mirror, and headed inside.

His excitement at seeing me was obvious, greeting me with a big smile and a warm hug, like we were old friends. He was wearing a pair of tan slacks with brown shoes and a white button-up shirt. Very business casual, but still nicer than you would expect for someone who owns a garage. I couldn't help but think it was for my benefit, and I did appreciate it.

Once in his office, we sat again in the same places, and I asked him, "How are you doing today? Feeling better I hope?"

"Yes, I'm much better today. I do want to apologize again for falling apart on you that way—it was a little embarrassing I must say."

"You're fine," I responded with a smile, "It's nice to see a man that isn't afraid to share his emotions, and you clearly loved your wife, which is sweet."

As I spoke, I watched his eyes drop down once more to my high heels and calves and couldn't help getting the sense he was a little disappointed that I was wearing such a long, buttoned-up dress today.

"So here are the documents for you to sign, let's get that out of the way so we can be done with business," I said as I opened the folder in front of him on the desk.

Once that was done, I left his copies on the desk and put everything back in my bag.

"Now, I'm starving … Why don't you take me to a late lunch, and we can talk for a little bit—maybe share a little more with me about how your wife would tease you," I said with a little wink before standing up.

"Okay," he said with an amused tone as he smiled and grabbed his keys from the drawer.

We made small talk about the beautiful weather and businesses along the street as we drove a couple blocks to a small cafe with an outdoor seating area. The gentleman that he was, he insisted on opening my door for me each time, although he wasn't getting to see very much with my dress buttoned almost to my knees. But playing the conservative role right now was all part of my plan.

At the cafe, I asked the hostess to seat us outside, and I pointed to a table at the back corner. There were only two other men, in suits, sitting outside so this table was semi-private.

I sat in the corner, and then Tom sat to my left. When we first sat down, as Tom was taking his seat, I slyly unbuttoned the next button at the bottom of my dress, just above my knees. Since he was at an angle beside me, he could see my lap from where he was sitting, but also the table was made of a thin metal pattern that could be seen through as well. It only took him a few minutes to notice, although by the look on his face he was doubting whether that button was already open or not.

We talked for a few minutes and placed our order. He got a burger, and I opted for a beet salad. As Tom placed his order and gave the menus back to the waiter, I took that opportunity to sneak open another button over my thighs. The lace tops of my stockings were still concealed, but only by about a half inch. I made no indication of what I did, I just continued talking and acting normally, waiting for him to notice.

It only took him a minute before I saw his eyes drop and a smile start to form on his lips.

He looked back up at me and said, "You seem to be having a problem with the buttons on your dress—they look like they're falling open."

Smiling and playing along, I acted surprised and said, "Oh my, sure does look that way. I guess there's no point in rebuttoning them, they'll just probably fall open again."

Smiling, I continued, "So tell me about the little games you and your wife would play. And you said stockings have always been your thing—what did you mean by that?"

I swear I could see a little shade of red come into his cheeks as I asked him that.

Clearly a little nervous, he began, "Well, I've always had a thing for stockings and high heels on women, as long as I can remember. I remember watchin' my teachers in school or even women walkin' down the street."

He continued, "I'd always imagine what they were wearing under their dresses or skirts. And then one day, I remember sitting in the library and Mrs. Trundle walked in and sat at a table across from mine. I remember staring at her legs under the table, nervous I was going to get caught, and straining to see anything I could."

I could tell he was fondly recalling this memory and that it left such an impression even so many years later.

"When she went to leave, one of her folders fell off the side of the table and the papers went all over the floor. I remember watchin' her cussing under her breath as she stood up and walked around the table."

A small smile formed on his lips as he continued, "She wasn't paying any attention to me or anyone else in the library as I watched her hitch her skirt up about four inches so she could stoop down to gather her papers. For the next thirty seconds or so, everything I fantasized about at that age was right there in front of me. She was stooping down in her black high heels, her dark tan nylon covered legs pointed in my direction, with her knees at least a foot apart."

I could tell he was picturing it in his mind as he conveyed the details, "I could clearly see the dark tops of her stockings, the bare skin of her thighs, all the way to a pair of white sheer panties that did nothin' to hide her small triangle of dark hair. Once she had everything back in the folder, she stood up and placed it on her pile of papers and then smoothed her skirt back down. To this day, I always wondered if she knew I was lookin'. I always imagined that she did and was letting me see."

"Wow," escaped my lips, "it sounds like that made quite an impression."

"You have no idea! It fueled my fantasies for quite a few years, and then when I started getting into my dad's Penthouse magazines and every woman was wearing stockings and garter belts—I was in heaven. So, you can only imagine how wonderful it was to have a beautiful wife who loved wearing them as well—and loved teasing me with them."

I put my hand on top of his and squeezed as I said, "I'm so sorry—it sounds like you had a wonderful relationship."

Just then, the waiter brought our food.

Our talk was a little lighter while we ate, but after we finished, I asked him again, "So, now tell me how your wife teased you, and what you did about it."

"Mostly it was just her findin' ways to flash me or open her dress and give me a peek—sometimes just sitting there with the top of her stockings exposed no matter who was around. That used to drive me crazy."

"I see, and when she would open her dress, what was it she would give you a peek of?"

As he talked, I turned my chair slightly, so I was facing him more.

"Hmm … You name it! I guess it depended on her mood or where we were—sometimes her panties, sometimes her bra, sometimes her bare breasts, sometimes … everything."

I smiled at him, bringing my right hand down to trace my long fingernails in little circles above my knee, saying, "That sounds daring, and fun."

I traced my fingers up the top of my stocking covered thigh to the next button, continuing to just stare at his face as I flipped it open with my thumb. My dress parted off my legs to the next button, now open several inches above the pink garter strap clipped to my stocking.

He sat there just staring at my legs, not even smiling, just appreciating. I couldn't help but notice the effect opening that button had on him. Clearly the garter strap on my stocking was his trigger as the outline of an erection was growing down his left thigh.

I think he was genuinely startled when the waiter walked up to take our plates and asked if we needed anything else. I just sat there, smiling and answering the waiter as he clearly noticed my legs. Tom was amused that I made no effort to cover my thighs.

I looked back at Tom and asked, "You still haven't told me what you would do when your wife teased you—did you just sit there and look?"

He smiled again, pausing before saying, "At first, I would just look—but then I just had to run my hands over her legs. Feeling the nylon under my fingertips would always be a huge turn-on for me."

I could tell he was getting more and more excited now, opening up and sharing more intimate details.

He continued, "And depending on where we were, I might work my hand up between her thighs—you might say trying to call her bluff—and see if I couldn't get a response out of her."

I have to say that at this point I was feeling rather playful myself. Slowly exposing myself to Tom was having the effect I assumed—but it was also having it on me.

His erection was now fully grown down his thigh, straining against the material of his slacks, and I could see the desire in his eyes. It was that reaction and the way he was looking at me, that I loved—that I desired—that I did all this for.

I leaned forward, reached over and took his hand, and placed it on my knee. I could see the look on his face as he slowly started to move his fingers over the sheer nylon covering my leg. I'm guessing he hadn't felt that since his wife passed. Abruptly, I brought my hand down to hold his, smiling as I saw our waiter approaching with the bill.

I looked at him and said, "Thank you," as he placed it on the table and took another look at my legs.

Tom took his hand from my knee to get his wallet out and laid a credit card down with the bill.

When he looked back, another button was open.

The first button I opened was barely noticeable, the second button showed a lot of my thigh, but still hid anything too provocative. The third button revealed the fantasy and confirmed stockings and a garter belt. The fourth button I opened removed all doubt. Since my legs were still crossed, my thighs met to hide my complete exposure, but the top of my sheer pink panties were now peeking into view.

Tom's eyes were moving between my lap and my face as I just sat there, proud of my little display.

The waiter came over and picked up the bill with the credit card, not saying a word, but clearly surprised before walking away. I didn't even look at him, I just continued to look at Tom.

Tom looked over his shoulder at the waiter as he walked away, smiling back to me and saying, "You're something else."

"I'm just wondering how long it's going to take him to run the card, and what he might see when he comes back."

With that teasing comment, I brought my hand up to the top button of my dress and opened it. It didn't really expose anything, but it was the thought that made it exciting.

Not wanting to encourage the waiter too much more, when I saw him walking back in our direction, I dropped my right hand down to rest it just over my panties.

After Tom signed the credit card bill and put his wallet back in his pocket, he turned his full attention back to me.

Time for my final tease ...

I gave a sultry lick of my lips, then moving my hand from my lap, I uncrossed my legs.

I looked down at myself, seeing the pink triangle of my panties now completely on display as the bottom of the dress was laid open revealing everything up to my hips.

Tom's body was blocking the view of the men sitting on the other side of the patio, and our waiter was nowhere in sight. I looked at him and asked in a playful voice, "Are you going to call my bluff?"

I then slowly slid my high heels apart on the concrete, and let my knees relax open about six inches. I too was getting really aroused now. To this point, it was all simple teasing, but now I was putting myself on display, letting him see all of me through the sheer pink nylon, and inviting him to touch me. I could feel my heart racing and a slight tremble in my body as I made myself sit there with my knees open, watching

45

him bring his right hand down and rest it against the inside of my right calf. He began to move it ever so slowly up to the inside of my knee and then push forward up the inside of my thigh. I felt a tingle go through me when the rough tips of his fingers moved past the tops of my stockings and continued higher over the sensitive skin of my inner thigh.

Finally, the tips of his fingers came in contact with the front of my sheer panties. He gently traced his fingertips up and down the crease in the middle of my panties, tickling my smooth skin through the pink nylon. He paused for just a second to look up into my eyes, clearly asking if that was okay in a nonverbal way. I just let my eyes close slowly for a second as I licked my lips and let out a seductive little sigh.

Then, with a hook of his finger, that only an experienced man could do so smoothly, the front of my panty was pushed to the side and his thick callus finger penetrated me. My mouth dropped open as a gasp escaped my lips, my right hand instinctively gripping his large muscular forearm. He leaned forward, intensely looking into my eyes, watching me tremble with broken breath escaping my lips, as he flexed his finger in and out of me. A few small moans escaped my throat and then I heard him say, "Maybe we should go back to my office now."

Without a word, I just quickly nodded my head in agreement. He made a few more deliberate thrusts with his finger before leaning back, leaving a slight trail of my wetness down the inside of my thigh as he pulled his hand away.

He stood up, then extended his hand to take mine as I stood. My dress relaxed down, now covering my panties, but still open more than enough to expose my stockings and garter straps as I walked. The two men glanced over at me and then did a double take when they caught a glimpse of my legs as I passed by them. Our waiter got his final peek as well when he thanked us on our way out.

In the car on the short drive back to Tom's garage, nothing was said, but his hand alternated between caressing my thighs and firmly rubbing me through my panties, pushing the sheer material in against me. By the intense look in his eyes, and the way his hand was moving on my body, I knew that as soon as we were behind closed doors, a year of pent-up sexual frustration was going to be unleashed.

CHAPTER THREE

Behind Closed Doors

When we pulled into the lot and parked, I began buttoning the bottom of my dress to walk in, but Tom stopped me saying, "It's okay, nobody's here, everyone left for the day.

He quickly unlocked the front door, then re-locked it once we were inside. Grabbing my hand, he pulled me along as he couldn't get into his office fast enough. As soon as we were inside, his strong forearms slipped around my waist and pulled me tight against his body, pressing his lips to mine. He was kissing me with the passion of a man who has been in the desert for weeks and finally getting water. It felt so incredibly erotic and sexy to be wanted—desired this badly by a man.

His hands started roaming my body, up and down my back and then cupping my behind through my dress. I broke away from the kiss and pushed his hands down, stepping back several feet away from him. He just stood there watching me as I brought my fingers up and slowly began unbuttoning the front of my dress.

When I opened the last button in front of my hips, my dress was still laying closed as I brought my hands up slowly and took hold of it in front of my cleavage, peeling it back to reveal my lingerie and stockings. Letting it fall back off my shoulders and slip off my arms, I draped it over the back of the chair to my side. I then brought my fingers back over to the front of my bra where I unclipped it and peeled it back, baring my naked breasts to him. He was just standing, mesmerized as he watched me slowly revealing myself.

I stepped back in front of him, bringing my fingers up to his face, holding his cheeks in my hands as I placed a soft kiss on his lips. I stepped back slightly, not saying a word, just licking my lips, dropping my hands to his chest, and then slowly tracing my fingers down his stomach as I lowered myself in front of him.

His impressive erection strained the material of his slacks, just inches in front of my face now. There was a small spot of wetness from his arousal starting to show through the material. I glanced up at him a few times as he was watching me unfasten his belt and the front of his pants with my thin fingers. Once I had his pants open, I hooked my fingers in the waistband and tugged them down over his thighs, allowing his erection to freely rise as if it knew exactly where it was about to be. I was squatting in front of him, the bare cheeks of my bum resting back on my high heels, my knees spread wide. My hands were in front of me, resting flat against his thighs.

Tipping my head back, I looked up into his eyes as I leaned forward, letting my mouth drop open to take the bulging head of his penis between my lips. I closed my lips around the base of the head, at the same time closing my eyes to allow myself to experience all the sensations, including the cool air in the room chilling the dampness on the front of my panties. The same chill moved over my body, making my nipples almost painfully hard, wanting to be pinched and caressed.

I could feel the warmth of his muscular thighs against the palms of my hands, but mostly I was aware of the throbbing against my lips and tongue. It was like I could feel his heart beating in the head of his erection. His warm, sweet tasting precum was mixing with my saliva as I circled the head with my tongue, acquainting myself with every contour and texture. I wanted to feel more.

Leaning forward, I slowly slid my lips down the rigid, bumpy shaft of his erection, feeling the head move over my tongue, and start to enter the back of my throat. I pulled back slightly, then pushed forward again a little further. Just as I had noticed his massive hands and thick fingers, the thickness of his shaft was just as impressive, straining my jaw as I worked to take every inch of him. Finally, my nose nestled against his short pubic hair as I heard a long low moan escape his throat. His engorged head pressed deep into the back of my throat as I held myself there, holding my breath, until finally pulling all the way off of him with a loud wet gasp.

I took a few short breaths, then wrapped both of my hands around the base of his shaft, sealed my lips around the head of it again, and began bobbing in and out as I stroked him with my hands. My efforts were met with a steady vocal chant of "Oh God ... Yes ... Yes, that's it ..."

He brought his hands down to lightly stroke my hair as I pleasured him with my mouth. After a few minutes of this, he pushed me back and then effortlessly lifted me up to my feet by my arms. Guiding me over to his desk, he cleared the middle and then directed me to lie on my back. His fingers quickly went under my hips, hooking the waistband of my panties and peeling them from under me, sliding them up my thighs and over my heels. He raised my legs and spread them open wide by my knees, lowering himself down to drive his tongue against me, passionately licking and probing.

He clearly was very experienced and talented at pleasing a woman. Within a minute, he had me gripping the edge of the desk with a steady cry escaping my lips as his tongue flicked relentlessly back and forth in just the right places. He continued this for several minutes, intent on giving me an orgasm. A sudden wave went through my body, my back arching, squeezing my thighs against his head, and crying out as warm spasms rippled through my hips. Before I could recover, he was standing in front of me, my legs together with my high heels straight up in the air. With an intense wave of pleasure, building off the oral stimulation he just gave me, his rock-hard erection slid into me, not stopping until his hips were pressed against the back of my thighs.

A loud cry escaped my lips, exhaling all the air from my lungs, as I felt a sense of sudden fullness.

Oh my God … He's so big!

He started into a steady rhythm, fully stroking himself all the way in and out of me. I was now letting out a little grunt with each of his deep thrusts, gripping the edge of the desk to keep from sliding away as he pushed into me. He had my legs together, extended straight up against his chest. His face was pressed against my ankles, no doubt feeling the sheer nylon against his skin. His left forearm tightly held my thighs to secure me against his thrusts, and his right hand was moving over my stocking covered legs.

After working himself through his frenzy, his intense thrusting now slowed to a gentle pulsing. He lowered my legs down to one side, turning my hips on the desk and twisting my torso as I kept my shoulders down facing him. He ran his hand over my hip and up my ribs, then began gently caressing my breasts. I looked up at him, smiling and content, all my needs met, and asked, "Can I make you feel good now? Let me take care of you."

He just smiled and nodded as he stepped back, slipping from between my legs. I pushed myself up on the edge of the desk, looking over at his hips. He was still just as hard, but now every inch glistened with my wetness. I turned sideways at the front edge of the desk, laying down on my side, pushing my hips back and pulling my knees up. Looking up at him, I extended my open hand, and said, "Come over here."

When he stepped forward within my reach, I closed my fingers around the base of his shaft and directed him to my mouth. Before taking him, I looked up and said, "This way you can caress my legs and let yourself go. Just feel my lips on you as you feel my stockings—and let go."

A relaxing sigh escaped his lips as I pulled him into my mouth. His hand immediately moved down my hip and began stroking every inch of my legs. It felt incredibly relaxing and sensual to me as well, his hands caressing my body while my lips massaged his shaft.

I could taste myself all over him—the sweet juices from my climax mixing with his. As I felt him start to get close, I slid my hand around his hip, pulling him forward to push deeper into my mouth. Suddenly, I felt his right hand stop moving on my thigh and squeeze firmly. His left hand came around to the back of my head, his fingers closing in my hair, holding me in place as he began to release.

I could feel his erection, as hard as it could be, the swollen head pulsing, releasing each jet deep into the back of my throat. I struggled to swallow as much as I could, trying not to choke as what felt like a year's worth of pent-up sexual tension was released. Once his orgasm began to subside, his hand released my hair and I slowly pulled back, keeping my lips sealed around the head. I continued to slowly stroke him as I tenderly sucked at the tip, getting every last drop before laying back onto the desk.

He stepped back, once again looking emotional, as he said in the sincerest tone, "Thank you, that was amazing—thank you so much for giving me that."

He stepped back further, reaching down to pull his pants back up as I pushed myself up off the desk. I smiled at him, and in an equally sincere tone, I said, "You are so very welcome. Believe me, it was my pleasure too," ending with a little chuckle.

I walked over to the chair where my dress was lying, my legs a little shaky and unsteady on my high heels. Slipping on my panties, and then my bra, I picked up my dress and wrapped it back around my body. I looked up at him as I finished buttoning the front and he was just standing there, watching me, with a smile.

I walked over and gave him a kiss on the cheek and stood in front of him with my hands resting on his chest, and said, "You know I'm married, I just wanted to do this special thing for you. I'm not looking for anything to continue. I hope you understand."

He smiled at me and brought his hands up to rub the outsides of my arms, saying, "You don't have to worry. Yes, I completely understand, and I appreciate everything you shared, and did for me."

He also added with a wink, "But of course, if you ever want to share again, you know where to find me."

I laughed and said teasingly, "Maybe ... I might just be driving around in my stockings and garter belt, and my car breaks down, and I'll know who to call."

"But in all seriousness, I really did enjoy sharing that with you, and I am going to be your sales rep. Perhaps I'll let you take me to lunch again."

I picked up my bag, gave him another kiss on the cheek, and he walked me out, unlocking the front door for me.

I've spoken with Tom many times since on the phone, and he's always been a gentleman and never pushed for more. Tom is a great person, and a wonderful customer. I do feel like I need to visit him again sometime, check on him, and see how he's doing. He deserves that.

CONFESSION TWO:

Exposure at the Trade Show

CHAPTER FOUR

Unexpected Assignment

Emails answered ... Calls returned ... Calendar updated for the next three weeks ... Bring on the weekend!

It was Friday afternoon, and I just finished my last call for the week and felt pretty good about everything. Life had been a whirlwind for several weeks, and I was really pushing at work to wrap up a lot of loose ends and be able to slow down at the end of the year and enjoy the holidays. Maybe even take a few days off.

There were only fifteen minutes left in the day when my boss called and said he wanted to see me in his office. He didn't sound upset or anything, but there was a slight tone of anxiety in his voice. When I got there, he proceeded to explain that they had a booth at a trade show in the coming week, but the woman who typically works the shows became sick and can't go.

Since in past years I'd had some experience working a few different shows, he wanted me to fill in for her. I wasn't exactly crazy about doing it, especially at the last minute like this, but I didn't really have much choice. He was telling more than asking. However, the good company girl I am, I smiled and said, "Sure, I can handle this, don't worry."

He sincerely thanked me for covering and said he would forward me all the details. Later that evening, I let my husband know about my unexpected trip. He was fine with it and understood things come up. Through the weekend, I went over the info for the conference, trying to get my head around the schedule, what I needed to pack, and understand the industry.

FABTEK, Georgia World Conference Center, connected to the Orion Atlanta Hotel. North America's largest metal forming, fabricating, and finishing event.

Honestly, my first thought was, *What the ...*

This was not at all an industry conference I would have imagined we would take part in, but I guess no matter what the industry, everyone has offices and needs supplies to run those offices. Our company recently appointed a new marketing director, and I guess he was trying to think outside of the box and find new angles to reach more businesses.

Okay then, I'll do my best ...

The event spanned three days throughout the week, but I had to leave on Monday to get settled in and make sure everything was set up. We had an advance team that took care of our booth, so all I had to do was show up, organize things, and look pretty.

Glancing through the schedule of events, obviously most of it was just working the floor at the booth, but there were also a couple of meet-and-greets, and a few twenty-minute presentation sessions to talk about our products and services to small groups.

Sunday night I packed for my week, or should I say, overpacked. Really not knowing what to expect, I had outfits for almost every occasion, but there was a definite theme— "sex sells".

There were no flats, sneakers, or sandals. Every shoe in my bag had at least a four-inch-high heel. There were no pants, only skirts and dresses, and nothing that fell below mid-thigh. Some with buttons that could be opened, some with daring slits, and some that loosely wrapped my body, just wanting to reveal. The few bras I packed were delicate and sheer. The panties were matching and barely there. Lastly was my lingerie and hosiery. I added a few pairs of stay-up thigh-highs and stockings, sheer-to-waist pantyhose, two garter belts, cream and black, and a few of my favorite nighties.

I wasn't naive to why they send an attractive woman to "man" a booth at a clearly male dominated industry event. I knew what I was there for, and in the back of my mind, the undeniable thoughts of being out of town and "letting happen what may happen" were there.

CHAPTER FIVE

FABTEK, Here I Come

After a rushed Monday morning, getting to the airport, and a fairly short and uneventful flight, I arrived in Atlanta. I always hated traveling but still tried to make the best of it. Well, I shouldn't say I hate traveling, I hate the getting there part. Especially when I'm by myself, having to wrangle my luggage, finding transportation, and just the general annoyances of getting into my actual hotel room.

Finally getting settled around four P.M., I had to find the exhibit hall and make sure our booth was all taken care of. It was quite a trek from my room to the hall, but I finally found it. I was relieved to see that we had a pretty good spot, and everything was ready to go. I only needed to load a couple slideshows and put out our literature.

I was in front of our booth, bending at the waist, fixing some of the front table skirting. Still in my traveling outfit, a comfy short gray cotton dress, sheer nude pantyhose, and black high heels, I was apparently giving quite the view of my behind and legs as I bent over. As I adjusted the skirting, I happened to glance back and noticed a few of the men down the aisle pausing to enjoy my position. Most of them were workers setting up stanchions and walkways, but one man in particular was standing off to the side with his arms crossed, and a little smile on his face as he stared in my direction.

I finished and stood back up, turning quickly to walk around the booth and looked right at him, making eye contact. Typically, in a situation like that, if I look right at a man after he's been staring at me, they look away or act as if they weren't doing anything. But not this guy, he was a little younger, well dressed in a white button-up shirt, slacks, and a sports jacket. He had wavy brown hair and somehow exuded confidence just standing there.

I gave a smirk, as if to say, "I know what you were looking at," and he smiled right back at me, continuing our duel. I'm usually the one who controls this little game, but there was something about him that made me feel I'd met a formidable opponent and surprised myself that I was the one to look away first.

Once inside my booth, I arranged some of the literature but stole a few more glances up in the direction of my admirer. He continued to watch me for another minute or so before giving a little nod in my direction with a smile and then turned to casually walk away.

I was honestly surprised at how I felt a little flustered from that brief exchange. I was smiling to myself and felt like the shy girl that just got noticed by one of the football players. I moved on, telling myself I probably won't even see him again, and turned my attention back to my booth.

CHAPTER SIX

Formally Meeting Aaron

Once back up in my room, I double checked the schedule. There was a kickoff cocktail party in one of the small banquet rooms for the show exhibitors, so I had to start getting ready. I selected an outfit and laid it out on my bed, then jumped in a nice quick hot shower, touched up my makeup and hair, then got dressed.

You only get one chance to make a first impression, so I wanted to be sure I looked my best as I mingled and networked through the crowd tonight. The rest of the show was for the public, and while many of them are business owners, my real targets are the larger companies taking part in the show that would be represented tonight.

I chose a short sleeve, red wrap party dress. Nothing seems to quite get a man's attention like a beautiful woman walking into the room with a red dress on. This dress was cute, and one of my favorites, falling just about mid-thigh, it flowed and teased as I walked, but the real draw was the deep cut V of the neckline the way it fell over my breasts. Many times, I've had to pin it between my breasts just to keep it from being too revealing for the occasion, but not tonight. I'll be holding my clutch in one hand and a drink in the other leaving the neckline to fall where it may. I finished the outfit with a black thong panty, nude stay-up thigh-highs, and a pair of black slingback high heels. The absence of a bra was evident where the material parted between my breasts as I moved. One last check of the mirror in the hallway, and I headed down to the party.

Walking through the lobby of the hotel, making my way to the banquet room, I could feel the eyes of the men all around me. Holding my head high, my shoulders back and letting my hips naturally sway with each step of my high heels, I felt confident and sexy. As I approached the open doors to the banquet hall, I remembered giving myself a pep talk.

Alright, I'm going to kill it this week, let's see how many new clients I can bring back and look damn good doing it.

I stepped into the room, standing for a moment to take in the lay of the land, and as I anticipated, getting the attention of many of the men. They still carried on with their conversations, but their eyes were looking in my direction.

First stop, the bar.

With a raspberry martini in hand, I began mingling through the room. Trying to read everyone, there were clearly three times as many men as women, which was good for me. The women, no doubt a few were owners or execs of companies, mostly were there like me, eye candy to reel in the big fish.

All the younger, handsome men in the room were sales reps or marketing guys sent by their companies. The middle aged and older gentlemen were usually VPs or owners. Those were the men I preferred to connect with. The younger guys were cute, but most had no real decision-making ability and would have to take things back to their bosses and usually don't.

I started making eye contact, smiling, and it only took a

71

minute before I was engaged in my first conversation. A distinguished man, salt and pepper hair, maybe late fifties, flattering me and flirting as he told me about his hydraulics company. He was pleasant, and it's always good to make connections, but he was only a single location business and not quite what I was looking to pitch to. We exchanged business cards and pleasantries, and I moved on.

Over the next forty-five minutes, I made at least a dozen more connections, some better than others, but all good. I just finished my second martini, and was feeling a mild buzz, and it seemed everyone else was feeling good too. You could tell the room had gotten a little louder, and there was a lot more laughter echoing throughout.

I immediately noticed a lot more hands beginning to roam over my back and around my waist as I would stand close to a gentleman I was talking to. And it was becoming blatantly obvious as I watched men's eyes dart from my face to my cleavage and back repeatedly. A couple times, I felt a hand drop to the top curve of my ass, one even grazing down across my cheeks. I made no acknowledgment and didn't miss a beat, enjoying the attention, but continue moving before they had a chance to push too far.

After finishing a very dry conversation about metal forming, I made my way back to the bar for my third martini. I had my drink in my hand and was turning, not paying attention as I tried to close my clutch with my other hand and bumped right into a man behind me.

"Oh my gosh, I'm so sorry!" just escaped my lips as I looked up, and it was him.

It was my admirer from earlier in the convention hall. We were literally inches away from each other, my head slightly tilted back as I looked up, his deep blue eyes seemed to pierce into my soul. His full lips formed into a knowing smile as he answered, "No worries, it's my fault also, I was probably standing too close."

Before I could answer, he continued, "I believe we met earlier, down in the exhibit hall."

Pulling my wits together, I responded, "Oh, yes, I do remember seeing you there, but I didn't think we met."

He smiled again, with his lips and a slight raise of his eyebrows, saying, "Well, I guess not formally, but it did feel like we shared a momentary connection."

A connection huh, I wonder if that was before or after I was bent over in front of you—but he's not wrong, we did share a connection.

I just smiled, and he continued, "Either way, my name's Aaron. It's a pleasure to make your acquaintance, formally."

"It's nice to meet you Aaron," I replied with a coy little smile.

He reached around my shoulder to the bar and picked up his drink the bartender set for him, bringing his face even closer to mine, and then said, "Why don't we go over to one of the tables and get to know each other a little better. I'd love to hear what you do and more about you."

With another subtle smile, I followed his lead across the room to a small high-top table next to the wall. Setting my clutch and drink down on the table, I slipped up onto the stool, hooking my high heel in the rung and crossing my legs.

He was wearing a gray tailored suit jacket and pants, with a fitted white button-up shirt underneath, no tie, and the top few buttons undone for a casual look. I couldn't help but think he bore some resemblance to Brad Pitt.

Aaron stood in front of me, close enough that the foot of my crossed leg was brushing the inside of his leg. It was such a subtle thing, but he made no effort to move, and I did the same, letting the side of my high heel continue to press against him.

Our conversation was very natural and effortless, as we shared our stories, about work and family. I assumed he was there as a representative of some company, but he was actually the owner of his own startup that had done very well. He was younger than me, having just turned thirty, single but dating a lot.

His company was based on a new technique of laser cutting for metal and fabrication and his business was growing quickly. Despite much of the conversation pertaining to work, I could still feel a flirtatious sexual tension between us. He didn't miss any opportunity to compliment me and subtly make me aware he was admiring the way my dress had parted open, exposing most of my thigh and just a slight indication of the lace band at the top of my thigh-highs.

I also returned my own subtle messages, occasionally flexing my ankle to brush the side of my foot an inch or so up and down on the inside of his knee. At one point, he made a comment about my earrings, saying that they were beautiful, and he noticed them because they looked like something delicate that had been cut by a laser.

As he said that, he moved his hand up by my cheek and

used his fingers to push my hair behind my ear, then slowly tracing the tip of his finger down around the outside of my ear until he was holding my earring out slightly. The touch of his finger tracing my ear was very sensual, and he knew that. He stared into my eyes, with a very intense look, until he moved his hand away. But he didn't just pull it out, his fingertips went to the nape of my neck and softly touched my skin, sliding them down to my shoulder, then pulling them away.

I'm not sure if he could see it, or feel it, but a shiver went through my body as he touched what is a very sensitive and erotic area. For the first time in our little dance, I showed signs of cracking, and he saw it. As his fingers slid from my neck, I felt my lips quiver and my breath catch, and then the corner of his mouth raised slightly, indicating a subtle smile and telling me that he knew he invoked a response.

Oh my ... He is good.

Most men go straight for the hand on the leg or on your behind, but Aaron ... he knew—he knew how to touch a woman. The connection with my foot against his leg, the way he stood close to me as we talked, brushing my hair back with his fingers, touching my ear and neck the way he did, he knew.

As we talked, we began sharing stories and experiences, and he told me about an accident he was in many years ago. He described how he was impaled by a thin metal bar in his abdomen. I responded, saying how terrible that was, and making a comment that it must have left quite a scar.

He said, "It did, there's still a mark. Here, feel it."

And with that, he unbuttoned a few buttons of his fitted shirt just above his belt and reached for my hand. I didn't say anything or stop him as he took my hand and slid it inside the opening against his stomach—his rock-hard, chiseled stomach. I think he saw me biting my lower lip as he slowly slid my fingers across his skin to his side under his shirt.

"Right here, can you feel that?"

He was slowly moving my fingertips in a small circle over what was clearly a scar on his side.

"Yes, I can feel it," I responded.

He slid his hand away, leaving my hand inside of his shirt against his stomach. I awkwardly left it laying there for a few seconds before slipping it back out, dragging my fingertips over the muscular curves. I clearly displayed my nervous response to having touched his bare skin under his shirt, reaching for my martini glass and anxiously taking a drink. His confidence was exuding from him as he knew he was establishing the dominant position with me.

Not used to the tables being turned, I'm usually the one making the man squirm and feel the warm arousal building inside of him. But I have to say, I was enjoying it. The trait that struck me the most with Aaron was his patience. He was taking his time, he wasn't trying to rush, and he knew he was building the desire in me. His patience became most exemplified with what he said and did next.

"It was wonderful getting to know you this evening, and I'm very much looking forward to spending more time together over the next few days."

And just like that, he picked up my hand and gave a soft kiss on the back of it, smiled, and walked away. No trying to go back to my room, no more drinks, no hand running up the inside of my thigh, just pushing all of my buttons and then leaving me sitting there feeling ... desire.

Once I was left alone for a few minutes, I began getting approached by other men. While I tried to turn my attention back to work, my conversations with them were half-hearted and distracted. Soon I called it an evening and made my way back up to my room.

I got ready for bed, slipping out of my high heels, untying my dress and laying it over the chair, then sliding my nylons down each leg. I slid one of my soft satin nighties over my head and let it fall over my body, then removed my thong panties and laid them with my nylons on the chair. Turning off the lamp and slipping between the sheets, I laid there replaying my interaction with Aaron this evening.

I replayed the things that he said, but then my mind drifted to the unspoken. I unconsciously began moving my fingertips over my body under the covers as I replayed the feeling of his touch on my ear, my neck, and my hand. I remembered the feeling of his warm skin under my fingertips as I slid them across his stomach, at the same time my fingers slipped between my legs under the covers.

I pushed my legs apart, bending my knees and opening my hips as I began tracing the tip of my middle finger up and down the soft shaved lips of my pussy. My left hand joined in caressing my body as I slid it over the slippery material of my nightgown, up to trace my breasts and run my fingernails over my nipples. Immediately, the stimulation of my sensitive nipples shot a tingle between my legs as I pressed the pad of my middle finger between my lips to caress myself.

God, I'm wet and aroused, went through my mind as I felt my finger slip effortlessly between my lips.

Replaying the touch of his fingers on my ear and neck, I began a slow circular motion with my finger over my clit, occasionally slipping it down to penetrate myself, then sliding my wetness back up to lubricate. I was amazed at how aroused I felt, laying there stimulating myself to the memory of an encounter with a man I just met and wasn't even that sexual, at least not physically.

Within a few minutes, I brought myself to an orgasm, pushing my hips open as wide as I could as I pressed my fingers into myself, arching my back, squeezing my breasts and nipples, all while a long deep groan escaped my gaped open mouth. As my orgasm passed, my body relaxed into the bed, and I didn't even remember falling asleep.

CHAPTER SEVEN

Day One

The next morning, I awoke surprisingly rested and ready to tackle the day. It was seven A.M., so I had plenty of time to get a shower, do my hair and makeup to look my best, grab a coffee, and get to my booth before the doors opened.

For the first day of the show, I was wearing a royal blue blazer dress. It was long sleeved, with four buttons in a square on the front, and fell just above mid-thigh. I wanted to show a lot of leg as I stood at my booth and this dress did just that. The top had a deep V cut to it the way it overlapped so I wore a black sheer and lace bra underneath that would peek out occasionally.

Because of the same shallow wrap at the bottom and no buttons below my waist, when I walk or sit, the dress would open with quite a tease of my upper thigh, so I wore a pair of nude sheer-to-waist pantyhose. Finally, I paired it with my tan, four-inch-high heel, Jimmy Choo pumps.

This outfit perfectly teetered on the line of looking professional yet still sexy. The tan color and height of the heels, paired with the short hemline of the dress and nude hosiery, made my legs look especially long. One last check of the mirror, then I gathered my things and headed out.

With my coffee in hand, I made my way to my booth. The way it was laid out, the entire front was open for people to walk in and the only place for me to sit was in the back corner at a small high table with two very high stools, so I was always on display.

The doors to the show opened and a surprising number of people started flooding in. I would have never imagined the traffic that comes through this show, but someone said it's around thirty thousand people.

Office equipment and supplies at a metalworking show were not the easiest to foster interest in. I tried engaging a lot of people as they walked by but was met with a lot of smiles and "no thank you", no matter how much they seemed to enjoy my look. If there was a little lull, I adopted a pose sitting on the stool, turned slightly to the side with one of my heels hooked in the bottom rung and my other leg extended straight to the floor. This position elongated my leg and flexed my ankle, also parted the bottom of my dress to reveal the inner thigh of my bent leg and garnered a lot of double takes and lingering visitors as they passed by.

I understand how these shows work, and I don't get discouraged, I know I'm looking for those few customers that are the right ones that will turn into ongoing client contracts. And the real focus of my attention is the other large companies here more so than the general public.

At one point, I was flattered but it was a little awkward when two very burly men came up and wanted to get a picture with me. They were both a foot taller than me as they pressed me between them for a photo. Not sure why they wanted the photo, but I smiled and obliged.

I do know that the way I had my arms extended behind them, the top front of my dress was pulled open more than it typically would be, so there was definitely a deep cleavage shot. I'm not sure which one of them it was, but when they stepped away, one of them slid his hand down over my behind, and with enough pressure to know it wasn't an accident.

I just finished talking to a father and son from a construction company when I turned to see Aaron walking down the aisle towards me through the people. We made eye contact, and he smiled, and I immediately felt a flutter go through my stomach which surprised me that I was feeling that.

As he walked towards me, I took a moment to appreciate his six-foot stature and was now able to see his forearms and biceps in the cream-colored, short sleeve polo he was wearing. I also enjoyed the subtle gold watch on his wrist and the look of his V cut build, accentuated by his shirt tucked neatly into his pants. His tan khakis, adorned by a brown leather belt, fit him well also, giving just the hint of a bulge that implied he might not be wearing underwear. Just as I was looking him over, I also noticed his eyes moving from my high heels, up my legs, and over my body.

He stepped into my booth, and this time he greeted me as if we were old friends, taking my extended hand in his but then pulling me in to give me a hug and light kiss on the cheek. I couldn't help but feel the strength of his arm pulling my body against his and notice the intoxicating smell of his cologne being this close against him. He stepped back and made an obvious look up and down my body, then commented, "You aren't messin' around, are you? You're trying to drive all the guys crazy here, make them want to buy something from you whether they need it or not."

I just laughed and told him I had been flirted with quite a bit today so far, especially since 95% of the people here are men. Then he made a more direct comment, "That dress makes me want to do a little more than flirt if I'm being honest."

I just smiled and replied with, "Oh really, do tell."

Not sure if he was going to call my bluff and say something, but just then a few people walked into my booth.

He looked over at them and then back at me with a smile and said, "First things first, how does seven work for dinner tonight."

I gave a look of surprise, since he presumed I would join him for dinner, but then smiled and simply said, "I think that'll work."

He lingered around while I spoke to the people in my

booth. After they stepped out, I returned my attention to Aaron. We set the plans for meeting later that evening, exchanged cell phone numbers, and continued flirting before I told him I had to leave in a little bit to give one of the 20-minute presentations. He asked where it was and said perhaps he'd stop in to listen, then gave me a little wink and walked away. I couldn't help but enjoy the way his khakis fit his hips and tight butt as he walked.

Trying to regain my focus, I turned my attention back to the men around my booth until it was time to go.

CHAPTER EIGHT

Revealing Presentation

I made my way to the small meeting room where they had rows of chairs, and a stage set up in front. Throughout the entire day, every vendor was given a time slot to get up and talk about their products and make a small presentation. Mine was at three-twenty.

I was standing in the back of the room, just as the woman before me was starting her presentation. There was an MC that kind of introduced each person and then moderated the presentations, asking them questions and leading the itinerary. The stage was about 2 to 3 ft high, with bright lights glaring from each side and the ceiling. In the middle of the stage was a small table with two chairs, the MC on one side and the person presenting on the other.

I listened as he introduced the woman and then watched her begin giving her spiel. Almost immediately, I couldn't help but notice when she sat down, and then again, each time she would cross her legs, with the bright lights on the stage and the height of the platform, she was giving everyone in front of her a clear view up her skirt!

Her hemline fell just above her knees, but the angle and bright lights did nothing to hide the repeated view of her white panties. For a few seconds I was thinking, *oh, how embarrassing—she doesn't even know …*

And then it hit me—I'm up next!

Oh shit! My dress is shorter—way shorter than hers … It already wants to part open when I sit … and I'm wearing sheer nude pantyhose with nothing underneath—I'm going to flash all these men!

I could feel a nervous flush going through my face and body as I stood there, trying to think how to handle this. I watched her finish up her presentation, exposing herself several more times before the MC took over and thanked her for her time. I heard him announce there would be a five-minute break and then heard my name as the next presenter. I made my way up to the stage, now more nervous than ever, as I carefully ascended the three steps up to the platform. The MC greeted me pleasantly and quickly touched on the points I wanted to go over, before turning back to his notes on the table.

I walked over to my chair and turned to look out at the audience. Most people were still shuffling around, but many were staying in their seats and intently watching the stage, no doubt anticipating what they were going to see. Because of the bright lights, and the rest of the room being dimly lit, it was hard to see the back of the audience. It was mostly the first few rows that I could make out, but they were close enough that I could see their expressions and tell where their eyes were looking.

There were several men patiently waiting in their seats that I could see their eyes darting up and down my legs and body, and I knew exactly what they were waiting for. Just before we were about to start, I saw Aaron making his way down to the front and watched him take a seat in the third row directly in front of me. I smiled and gave a little wave to him, now even more nervous that I was going to be exposing myself to him as well. But as nervous as I was, I couldn't help feeling a growing arousal knowing I was going to be so intimately on display.

I took a deep breath and stepped over in front of my chair, then squeezing my knees together and placing a hand in the middle of my dress where it overlapped, I lowered myself into my seat. Almost in unison, I watched the first three rows of men directly in front of me drop their eyes to my legs as I sat down. I started off well, sitting ladylike with my shins at an angle and my knees together. As my presentation went on though, I naturally started using my hands when I talked, and became slightly more animated, shifting in my seat.

At this point, I realized I was probably only slightly showing glimpses between my thighs and doing a fairly decent job of concealing myself, but a little voice inside dared me. I couldn't help but notice Aaron intently watching me, along with fifteen or twenty other men of all different looks and backgrounds. As I gave my talk on autopilot like so many times before, I couldn't deny the voice in the back of my mind that continued to dare me to at least once carelessly cross my legs in front of all of them.

It was almost as if I felt myself do it from outside my

body, straightening myself up in my chair, continuing to talk as I let my knees relax ever so slightly, then cross my right leg over my left. With a split-second glance down, I saw the bottom of my dress parted over my thigh, exposing as much of my thigh as it possibly could. Typically, I would have no way of knowing what a man in front of me saw when I crossed my legs in his direction, but in this case, I felt like I had twenty mirrors in front of me, the faces of all those men clearly reflecting what I just exposed to them.

I saw eyebrows rise, eyes get wider, mouths slightly drop open, and intense focus toward my knees. I then looked at Aaron, and he had a calm smirk on his face.

I've stood in front of a mirror in nothing but my sheer nude hose, there is nothing hidden. And the style of hose I was wearing did not have a cotton gusset sewn in, only a thin seam from front to back, doing nothing to conceal. I might as well have been naked. Getting an undeniable rush from what I just did, I thought to myself, *I'm never going to see these men again, and when am I ever going to have a chance to do something so naughty in such an "accidental" way.*

With that, my presentation was wrapping up. The MC began to speak, thanking me and making announcements as I took a deep breath and then slowly uncrossed my legs, sitting for a few seconds with my knees parted slightly more than they needed to be directly in Aaron's direction. I was doing this for his benefit, but the men all around him were fortunate enough to share in the gift I was giving him. Although I was doing it on purpose, I didn't acknowledge that he was looking or could see. I acted distracted and gathered my notes. I could feel a warm rush and slight tremble going through my body as I held that position. My breathing was shallow and all I kept thinking was, *I'm letting them see me, all of me.*

If it was possible to feel the weight of someone's stare, I felt it then. After what felt like several minutes, but really only a few seconds, I pushed myself up from the chair and smoothed my dress down, then walked off the stage. Aaron met me at the back of the room and immediately told me what a great job I did. I gave no indication that I knew what I had just exposed to all of them, only telling him how nervous I was being up on stage and speaking.

That was mostly a lie, I normally have no trouble speaking in front of groups and usually enjoy it, the nerves came from the situation. A few other men passed by that I recognized from sitting directly in front of me, telling me I did a "great job" and "wonderful presentation".

I wonder if they heard a single word I said, I thought, laughing to myself.

Aaron walked with me back to my booth, making small talk and occasionally letting his hand brush up and down my back. He told me he was really looking forward to dinner but had to run to a couple meetings beforehand. I smiled and said I was looking forward to it as well, and then to my surprise, he leaned in and gave me a kiss on the lips. It wasn't too long, but long enough to not be just a quick peck. Long enough to feel his soft, full lips pressed into mine. Long enough to feel his hands move down my ribs to grip the outside of my hips firmly. Long enough to let my eyes drop shut and feel my body begin to melt.

Just as suddenly, he pulled away, flashing that coy smile of his and said, "I'll see you tonight."

Recovering from the unexpected kiss, I finished out the afternoon in my booth, anxiously anticipating the evening to come.

CHAPTER NINE

Meeting in the Lobby

The exhibit hall was still open, and people were milling around, but I was done for the day, my mind was elsewhere. I wanted to get up to my room to have plenty of time to pamper myself and look nice for my dinner date.

After my shower, taking a little extra time on my makeup and hair, I walked through my hotel room naked. Going to the closet where I hung all my dresses, I knew the exact one I wanted to wear. It was a black halter top that tied behind the neck, deep cleavage with just the hint of the outside of my breasts exposed. The material was soft and flowing and it fell a few inches above my knees. Underneath were the skimpiest pair of sheer black G-string panties, matching black garter belt, and black stockings. I only wear a garter belt with stockings on special occasions and it's not something that I'm accustomed to having on, so when I do wear one, it feels especially sexy under my dress to me. The shoes were a pair of black, Steve Madden, very high-heeled pumps. I finished the outfit with some silver bracelets, a thin necklace and a cute pair of dangly, sparkly earrings. The halter top conformed to my breasts, exposing just enough, and allowing my nipples to clearly poke through the material in the most subtle teasing way.

To this point, my interactions with Aaron were purely flirtatious. I knew tonight was going to cross that line.

I stepped off the elevator and made my way into the lobby where Aaron was sitting off to the side waiting for me. He looked even more handsome, now wearing a very nicely fitted black suit with a white shirt and blue and gray print tie.

As I approached him, he stood up to greet me. He took my hands in his and spread my arms wide, saying, "Wow, you look amazing."

"You look pretty good yourself," I responded with a smile.

I continued, "So where are we going for dinner?"

"Before we go, have a seat, I'd like to talk for a few moments."

His demeanor seemed to change slightly, still pleasant but a little more serious.

Trying to stay light, I said, "Of course, what would you like to talk about?"

"I'm one who believes in clear communication, and I don't want anyone doing anything they don't want to."

"I agree, I feel the same way."

"So, before we go any further with this little game that we're playing, I need to know that you are comfortable with where this evening will most likely take us."

I paused for a moment, a little surprised at his bluntness but respected his honesty. He just sat there with an intense look, waiting for my response.

"Yes, I'm comfortable with it."

A smile formed on his lips, and he shifted in the seat next to mine, looking down at my legs and then back up to my face and said, "Uncross your legs."

I know my expression conveyed a look of confusion and surprise, but after a short pause, I uncrossed my legs, placing my high heels next to each other on the floor, sitting upright in my chair with my hands flat on each armrest. He was looking intensely into my eyes, a slight smirk on his lips as he asked me, "Do you like the idea of being submissive to a strong man? Giving yourself to him, letting him command you?"

I swallowed and felt my breath getting shallow as I thought to myself, *What am I getting myself into here? Am I ready to do this? What does he mean by all of that?*

The intensity and eroticism of the moment, along with my curiosity made my decision for me.

"Well, do you like that idea?"

My voice felt like it was ready to crack as I licked my lips and answered, "Yes ... Yes, I do."

This was like nothing I'd ever experienced with any other man. It was like something from a movie or erotic novel. I've been with men before who were rough, or aggressive, but that wasn't the way Aaron came across. It was an intense confidence with a calm, commanding demeanor, and it was incredibly erotic to think of surrendering myself to him this way. I was caught up in the moment and wanted to experience it.

Leaning forward slightly, he simply said, "Good, relax your legs."

And at his command, I let my knees drift apart as I looked down and watched him bring his hand up and slip his fingers slowly between them. Agonizingly slowly, he pushed his hand forward, further between my thighs, under the hem of my dress as I nervously looked around the room to make sure no one was watching.

My attention was drawn back to him as I heard him ask me, "Were you aware of what you did this afternoon?"

"What ... What do you mean?" I said nervously, but having a guess as to what he meant.

His hand pushed a little further between my thighs, his fingertips now on the lace tops of my stockings as he clarified, "This afternoon when you gave your presentation, were you aware of what you did?"

I felt nervous and embarrassed to answer honestly as I said, "I'm not sure I know what you mean, what did I do?"

Leaning forward a few more inches, he pushed his fingertips over the bare skin of my inner thighs above my stockings, again asking, "Were you aware that you showed a room full of men your pussy?"

As that last word left his lips, he pushed his hand forward and pressed his fingertips against me through the front of my sheer panties. The width of his hand parted my legs even further. A light gasp escaped my lips as I felt his fingers begin to move against me, sitting right there in the lobby of the hotel.

Again, I nervously scanned the lobby before looking back at him as he sat there staring at me with a smile, caressing me and saying, "Well?"

I sat there looking into his eyes as I felt his strong fingers pressing the thin sheer front of my panties between my smooth shaved lips. I squeezed the arms of the chair with my fingers, my eyes dropped closed for a second, as he gave a few firm thrusts of his finger.

Opening my eyes and taking a breath, I looked him in the eye and answered, "Yes, I knew they saw me—I knew you saw me. I did it on purpose, for you."

The smile on his face got bigger as he gave a final flex of his finger against me and then slid his hand from between my thighs.

"I thought that was the case, but I wanted to be sure. And that's what I based my hunch on, that you would be open to ... 'Playing', with me."

And with a little pause and final smile, he pushed himself up to his feet, extended his hand for mine and said, "Now, let's go to dinner."

CHAPTER TEN

Appetizer, Dinner, and Dessert

Walking beside Aaron through the lobby, hand in hand, I could feel the material of my panties moving against me with every step where he pushed them into me. There was nervous excitement swirling in my body, my mind racing through what he just said to me and what it all meant.

As we exited the front of the hotel, he led me over to a large black limousine that was waiting for us. The driver opened the door for us, and we climbed into the back, finding a spacious area with blue and white LED lights, a large couch like seating, and a fully stocked mini bar.

Aaron made us both a drink and then sat down close beside me. As we sipped them, he shared a little more with me about what he likes, and what he likes from a woman. He told me how he admires my confidence and the way that I carried myself, but mostly the way I understand the nuances of flirting and teasing. After the cocktail party, he felt confident that I was a woman that would appreciate his style of flirtation and be willing to handle, and even embrace his desires in the bedroom, and out of the bedroom. I'll admit, it was a lot to take in and clearly pushed my level of comfort and experience, but I also felt alive and excited to explore where he planned to take me.

He stopped talking for a few seconds, just staring at me, then said, "There's something I need to do, something I've wanted to do since I met you, and especially after your presentation this afternoon."

And with that, he took my drink from my hand and set it to the side, turned back toward me and slipped his forearm under the back of my calves, picking my legs up and spinning me sideways in the seat. I fell back slightly, catching myself on my elbow as I watched and felt him part my legs by my ankles, then run his palms up my shins and over my knees, pushing them open.

Shocked at the position he was putting me in, I asked, "What are you doing?"

He paused for a second and looked up at me, asking a question of his own, "Your body's mine tonight, right?"

A nervous, "Yes," escaped my lips.

With no further warning, my dress was up around my hips exposing my stockings, garter belt, and panties. He hooked his fingers in the front and pulled my panties to the side, then quickly leaned down to press his lips against me.

"Uhhhh ..." escaped my throat as I felt his tongue slip in between my lips and began flicking feverishly over my clit.

As he licked and kissed between my legs, I dropped my head back, my eyes closed and my mouth open. Propping myself up with my right arm, my left hand dropped down to the back of his head, sliding my fingers into his hair, I ground my hips against his mouth. After a minute or so of just using his tongue, I felt his finger slip up into me as he began stroking it in and out while he flicked his tongue across my clit. It all felt so wonderful, I was moaning out loud and pulling his lips tight against me as I felt an orgasm beginning to form.

I was so lost in what he was doing, I barely even noticed the car came to a stop. He pulled his lips away from me, sliding my panties back in place to cover me, and then sat up. I barely got my feet back down to the floor and was sliding my dress down as the door to the car opened for us to get out. Again, the expression on his face was one of confidence and pride in his performance. He was truly enjoying toying with me, and I must say I was enjoying it as well.

Once in the restaurant, they needed a minute to prepare our table, so we headed over to the bar for a drink. There was one empty stool at the end of the bar that I sat in, and he stood beside me. Aaron ordered two martinis for us while we waited, and then casually slipped his hand under the hem of my dress to caress my inner thigh.

"Did you enjoy what I did to you in the car?"

"No, it was terrible, I can't believe you made me endure that," I responded in an offended tone, trying to be funny.

He just smirked at me, and then I said with a wink, "I plan to put you through the same torturous experience, just so you know."

Just then the bartender set our drinks down. My eyes opened wide when I took the first sip, thinking, *did the*

106

bartender put anything in this except alcohol?

Once at our table, we enjoyed a delicious dinner, and two more martinis. While still sexually charged, some of our conversation covered a little more personal background and desires in life. He questioned my happiness at home and, knowing I was married, why I felt the need to explore. With the truth serum of vodka in me, my answers were probably a little more honest than they should have been.

"I'm happy in my marriage, and in my life, but … I just … I need to feel alive, and sexual, and desired. I want to feel daring. You know, do some things that are outside my comfort zone sometimes."

Aaron looked deep in my eyes and asked, "So what I said earlier, about being submissive, giving yourself to me, letting me direct you, does that excite you? Does that make you feel alive and sexual and desired?"

I paused a second, licking my lips and biting my bottom lip before answering, "Yes, that does sound exciting, and a little scary—but exciting."

He just sat there smiling at me, but I could see the thoughts going through his head. I could tell Aaron was starting to feel his drinks by the way his hand was roaming up and down my thigh under the table, but he still was nowhere near as intoxicated as I was getting. At 120 lbs., after finishing my fourth drink this evening, I was feeling no pain for sure.

Once back in the car, our thoughts and attention turned back to pleasure. With inhibitions being suppressed by the drinks in the car and those through dinner, I was prepared to give in to my sexual desires, and his.

The car began to move, and Aaron and I were embracing, kissing passionately as our tongues danced between our lips. My hand dropped to the inside of his thigh and slid up slowly until I felt his erection straining down his leg. My fingers barely closed over it as I began to stroke him through the material of his pants, impressed with his size and beyond ready to feel it, all of it.

I was going to return the favor on him during the drive back, ready to get on my knees between his legs, but he stopped me, saying, "Not yet, sit across from me."

I carefully moved to the seat opposite him and sat back, asking, "Now what?"

He looked so intense, staring at me as he said, "Show me your breasts."

I didn't hesitate as I slid my fingers up under my hair to the back of my neck, untying the straps of my halter. Once it was open, I slowly brought my hands down in front of my body, lowering the material to my waist and exposing my breasts for the first time to him. I sat there, my hands down to my sides, letting him enjoy my exposure as I felt little shivers go through my body putting myself on display like this. He sat quietly for a few seconds, just looking at me, then I heard him say "Your breasts are beautiful. Caress them."

I slowly slid my hands up from my waist, cupping my 34B breasts from underneath and squeezing them up together. I traced my fingers around my curves and then up to the front where I teased myself with my fingernails, raking them back and forth over my stiff nipples.

Aaron leaned over and pressed the button to talk to the driver, telling him to find a place to park for about ten minutes. Immediately I thought that we were going to have sex in the back of the car, but apparently, I was mistaken, as Aaron had a different plan to test my resolve.

I could feel the car maneuvering into a lot or somewhere as Aaron continued to watch me and said, "Take your dress off."

The car was stopped now as I stood up and pushed my dress down over my hips, letting it fall around my ankles, then sitting down and slipping it over my high heels.

"Toss it over to me," was his next instruction.

I did as he asked.

"Now, open your legs wide, and touch yourself for me."

All I could think was, *I've never done anything like this for anyone but my husband.*

It was embarrassing, but it felt so exciting that he was telling me to do it for him right here in this limo. I dropped my hand down between my legs and began rubbing myself through my panties while I brought my other hand up to my breasts and rolled my nipple between my thumb and forefinger.

I moved my hand inside of my panties and was starting to get myself incredibly aroused, getting into my performance for him when I heard him say "Don't stop, understand?"

I nodded to him, but he wanted to hear me answer him, "Say it, I want to hear you say it."

Through my heavier breathing, I said, "I understand."

And with that, I watched him reach over with his hand and press the button that lowered the privacy window between us and the driver. Aaron looked back at me, smiling at my nervous embarrassment and the look of surprise on my face as he repeated, "Don't stop."

I was physically trembling as I willed myself to keep my legs open and continue moving my fingers on my most intimate areas. I glanced over with just my eyes to see the driver turning his head to look back in through the window at me.

Aaron yelled up to him, "She wanted to show you how much she appreciated you driving us tonight," and then gave a little laugh.

The driver had a huge grin on his face, and he nodded his appreciation, then just stared at me as I continued my exhibition.

Over the next ten minutes, the two of them just sat there, quietly watching me as I worked myself to an orgasm. For the first few minutes, I had my eyes closed and wasn't thinking about being watched, but then something in me wanted to see their expressions, see how they were looking at me. I mainly focused on Aaron, but I couldn't help making eye contact a few times with the driver, feeling an incredible rush of embarrassed excitement as I performed such an intimate act in front of a stranger.

I can only imagine what he thought of me, sitting there with my knees pushed open wide in my high heels and stockings. My hand buried inside of my panties, frantically circling and thrusting my fingers into myself—my other hand caressing my breasts and rolling my nipples between my fingers—all while my mouth gaped open, gasping for breaths in between moans of pleasure until my entire body began to shutter with an orgasm right there in front of them.

Aaron sat intensely watching me, his hand slowly massaging himself through his pants. The driver was not as subtle. Although I could only see his head and shoulders, I could see his body rocking from the motion of his arm and hand, clearly masturbating openly to my show.

As my orgasm was subsiding, Aaron yelled up to the driver to take us back to the hotel now, and he put the privacy window back up.

Tossing my dress back over to me he said, "You were amazing. I hope you got a thrill out of that; I know I did."

"I can honestly say I've never done anything like that in my life, so thrill is a little bit of an understatement," I confessed.

We arrived at the hotel just as I finished tying the top of my halter dress behind my neck. It was awkward and embarrassing as I had to walk past the driver, shyly smiling at him as I made my way out of the car.

When I passed him, I said, "Thank you." with a tremble in my voice.

He nodded to me and replied, "No, Ma'am, thank you!"

Aaron was behind me, tipping the driver, then stepped up to put his arm around my waist to walk inside.

CHAPTER ELEVEN

Suite Surrender

We walked through the lobby towards the elevators, but there was a line of people that had just checked in apparently. Feeling a little disoriented from the alcohol, and everything rushing through my mind that I just did, I excused myself to slip into the ladies' room for a minute. I stepped out of the stall and over to the sink, putting my hands on the edge to steady myself as I looked in the mirror.

What are you doing? Are you sure you want to go up to his room? What's he going to be like? Am I ready for this? I interrogated myself standing there.

I was honestly doubting whether he was going to be too

much for me, both physically and psychologically.

I continued thinking, *He's clearly a little younger than me ... Strong ... Big ... Horny ... Kinky.*

My drunken confidence kicked in.

Fuck it! I'm going to rock his world, or he's going to rock mine, either way.

With a deep breath, I smoothed my dress down over my body and turned, doing my best to walk out like a classy, sober lady. The line at the elevator had dwindled as Aaron took my arm and led me over. The next elevator arrived, and Aaron and I stepped inside, followed by one older couple and four men who looked like they just returned from a day of golf. I was standing in the middle of the back, Aaron was in the corner to my left, the group of guys was in front to my right and the couple to the left. The couple were standing with their backs to us, just looking at the wall, but the group of guys were talking and facing in our direction. Everyone had pushed the buttons for their floors. I did make note that when Aaron leaned up and pushed the button, it was for the top floor.

The door started to close, and I heard Aaron say "Whoops," and looked down to see he dropped his key card.

I realized he did it on purpose when he stooped down to get it and then put his right hand on the inside of my calf. I nervously looked around to see if anyone was watching as I felt him slide his hand up between my legs from behind as he stood up. Once he was standing all the way, the back of my dress was bunched up on his forearm as he cupped the exposed cheeks of my ass in his palm, his two middle fingers hooked down between my legs and flexing up against me through my thin panties.

I swallowed and tried to look calm as he gave a little jerk with his arm, slightly knocking me off balance to the side and causing me to spread my feet. Once my feet were parted further, he had room to work his fingers inside of my panties and begin to penetrate me.

Sober I would have had a hard time not moving, but in my drunken state, the flexing of his wrist, and curling of his fingers into me caused me to sway forward and backwards ever so slightly, and I know the expression on my face was not hiding it either. My eyes were slowly closing and opening when I looked over and noticed one of the men was watching me. I kept thinking to myself that he didn't know, he was just looking at me, but then I saw him nudge the guy beside him and nod in my direction. I didn't look back at them, I just stared straight ahead, doing my best to hide the feeling emanating through my body from between my legs.

I looked over at Aaron briefly, and he was just staring straight ahead, as if nothing was happening. After the couple got off the elevator, the doors began to close, and Aaron began flexing his fingers harder and deeper into me. I wasn't hiding much of anything now, my body rocking from my hips with each of his hand movements. I didn't turn my head but just glanced over with my eyes and briefly made eye contact with the two men that were looking at me.

One of them smiled at me. Embarrassed, I quickly looked up and away, but that was followed by my eyes dropping shut and my lips parting as Aaron thrust his fingers a little deeper. When the elevator stopped at their floor, Aaron intentionally rocked my body forward and backward a couple times very noticeably, reflected in both my movement and my facial expressions. As the doors opened and the men began to step out, the one who smiled looked over at Aaron and said, "Have fun tonight!"

Aaron just turned and smiled, saying an energetic, "Thanks, I plan to!"

As soon as the door closed, I looked up at him and said, "Oh my God, you're so bad!"

He looked back at me smiling, and retorted, "Hey, at least I didn't invite them back to the room with us. Maybe next time though."

I just shook my head as he gave a few more thrusts of his fingers between my legs and then slid his hand away.

I didn't say anything, but I couldn't help but think, *Was he serious? I bet he was, I bet he would do that.*

The elevator door opened, and he led me to a large door to the left. There were no hallways, just a lobby area and a few large doors. Opening the door for me, he held it as I walked into his room.

Wow, was all I kept thinking.

It was a penthouse suite, bigger than most people's apartments or houses. I knew Aaron did well, but apparently, he did really, really well. I walked towards the center of the room between several large white couches, looking out through the wall of glass over the city.

"This is amazing!" I said as I turned to Aaron right behind me.

"Yeah, it's pretty nice, but you know what would make it

even more amazing?"

Without another word, he stepped forward and slid his hands behind my neck, untied the halter of my dress, and let it fall, draping around my waist.

"There. Now it looks so much better," he said before stepping forward and taking me in his arms to kiss me.

I could feel my naked breasts rubbing against his shirt as his hands moved over my back, up under my hair to caress my neck. He dropped his other hand down to squeeze my ass and pull my hips against him as his tongue darted into my mouth.

I slid my hands from his chest down over his ribs to his hips, pushing mine back slightly to make room as I worked the buckle of his belt open, then the button of his slacks, and finally his zipper down. Peeling the top of his pants open, I thrust my hand down into them, closing my fingers around his massive erection. Jerking my hand up and down from my elbow, I worked the shaft in my palm.

I was so aroused, feeling the warm skin of his penis finally against my hand, his tongue pushed into my mouth as I wrapped my lips to suck it. I heard a few low grunts escape his throat as I jerked down on his erection. He suddenly broke the kiss, looked deep into my eyes for a few seconds before he pushed down on my shoulders, and directed me where to go.

I lowered myself to my knees in front of him, hooking my fingers in the waist of his pants and slowly pulled them down to his thighs. His beautiful penis was swaying right in front of my face, hard and throbbing with the pulse of his heart. I had felt it with my hand, but seeing it in front of me, he looked so big. I looked up at his face for a second, licking my lips and running my hands over his bare thighs and hips before bringing them in to wrap my fingers around the base.

He was shaved smooth everywhere. The bumps and ridges of his shaft were pronounced, and the swollen head had a deep red color with a drop of precum glistening at the tip. Using my fingers to raise the tip, I parted my lips and leaned forward, feeling the head slip in over my tongue and tasting him for the first time. Almost in unison, a moan escaped both of our throats, his from the pleasure of my warm, moist mouth, mine from the anticipation of feeling him and pleasuring him so intimately.

With both of my hands wrapped around the lower part of his shaft, I began pumping him in and out of my mouth, my lips sealed around the head and my tongue dancing circles

121

over the tip. I teased him this way for several minutes, occasionally dipping him into the back of my throat as I adjusted to his girth.

He began getting more and more aroused, his hands moved into my hair, and he began to direct my movement as he stroked himself in and out of my lips. Showing him my submissive side, I moved my hands from his shaft and placed them flat on his thighs, giving him complete control of my movements and mouth. Slow but steady, he began stroking himself deeper and deeper into my mouth, pushing into the back of my throat, testing my limits.

I was no stranger to pleasuring a man orally, but he was definitely the largest I'd ever experienced. A few times my body convulsed as he touched the back of my throat, but soon his entire length was sliding smoothly in and out of my lips. Abruptly, he slipped out of my mouth and released my hair, stepping back as he frantically worked to unbutton his shirt. I stayed in my position on my knees, catching my breath from the deep oral I was giving him.

He was just staring at me as he removed his shirt, then his shoes, socks, and pants. The look in his eyes was slightly different now, more lustful, and a little intense. His large, naked, muscular body towered over me as he stepped forward, reaching down under my arms and picking me back up to my feet like I weighed nothing.

Again, he passionately kissed me as his hands pushed my dress down over my hips to my thighs where it fell around my high heels. Awkwardly stepping out of my dress, he pulled me by the hand over to one of the couches. Standing me in front of him, he sat down in the middle of one of the couches, spreading his knees wide and looking up at me, saying, "Suck me baby."

Returning to my knees, I leaned forward over his hips and lowered my mouth back around the head of his penis. He just sat back, his hands out to his sides, his head back and relaxed as he let me pleasure him. I slowed my pace back down, taking my time as I explored every ridge and bump with my tongue and lips.

Taking the head in my palm, I began milking the tip with my thumb and forefinger, feeling his precum lubricating my fingers as I worked him. My head was now down between his thighs, my lips gently suckling at his balls as I caressed them in my mouth with the tip of my tongue.

A steady stream of, "Oh fuck ... Oh yeah ..." escaped his

lips in a whisper-like tone.

Moving my mouth back up to the head, I began bobbing on him, occasionally making a loud, wet pop as the tip escaped my lips. When I increased my pace, his hands returned to my hair, once again pulling my head down to impale me on his manhood. Several times he held his entire length deep in my mouth until I began to squirm, then lifting my head to let me take a deep breath before thrusting himself all the way back in.

This game of taking my breath away went on for a few minutes before he released me. Sitting back on my high heels, I caught my breath as he leaned forward to fondle my breasts. He laid back onto the couch again, spreading his arms out wide. His erection showed no sign of losing its grandeur as it stood straight up between us, glistening and slightly swaying as if to charm me.

Aaron broke the silence, "Come up here and fuck me."

Placing my hands on his knees, I pushed myself up to my feet, then one leg at a time, I stepped over his to straddle him on the couch. Leaning over to one side, I reached down and pulled the front of my panties over to expose my pussy, then took his shaft in my hand and guided the tip against my lips.

He stopped me when he asked, "Do I need a condom?"

Not wanting to lose any of the intensity of the moment, I quickly said, "No, I can't get pregnant—just fuck me."

And with that, I guided the tip between the lips of my pussy and then slowly lowered myself down on to him. It felt like all the air was pushed out of my lungs as he penetrated me, so deep, stretching me around his shaft.

"Aaaahhhhhh," escaped my throat as I placed my hands on his shoulders to steady myself and adjust to his size.

He moved his hands to the outside of my thighs, running them up and down my stockings, then up to the bare skin of my hips and back down again. I could feel small thrusts from his hips as he began pushing upward into me. I responded by rolling my hips on him, now accustomed to his penetration. A steady exchange of grunts and moans began filling the room as our pace quickened. I was now bouncing on his lap, dropping my hips down onto him to maximize the penetration. His hands were moving over my body, squeezing my hips and the cheeks of my ass, or up to maul my breasts and pinch my nipples.

Suddenly, he sat forward, wrapping one arm around my waist. He pushed himself to the edge of the couch and then stood up holding me attached to him, impaled on his erection. I threw my arms up around his neck to support myself as he walked us across the room to a table.

Leaning forward, he sat me on the edge and then I laid back. I shivered for a second as the cold hard surface came in contact with my exposed skin. He was still inside of me as he ran his hands down the outside of my legs, hooking my calves and picking them up into the air. He slid his hands down a little further to grip each of my ankles and then extended my legs, spreading them wide up in front of him, putting me on display.

My feet in my high heels, and my stocking covered legs were spread in front of him as he looked down at me, watching himself slowly stroke the full length of his shaft in and out of me. I brought my hands up to my breasts, fondled them, caressing and pinching my nipples as he fucked me.

He continued to hold me in this spread position, slowly rocking his hips as he said, "Play with your pussy."

Without hesitation, I slid my right hand down over my stomach in between my legs. I pushed my fingers down to glide along his shaft as he slid in and out of me, I gathered our wetness and moved it up to my clit where I began making small circles with the pad of my middle finger. I can't describe how incredibly good it felt to tease my clit as his shaft slid in and out of me, the head hitting all the right places deep inside.

It was only a matter of a minute or so before an orgasm rippled through my body. I cried out as my back arched on the table, but he held my legs tight keeping them spread in the air as he drove deep into my pussy. My body relaxed, errant shocks convulsed through me, and he lowered my legs down and stepped back, sliding out of me.

Slowly I pushed myself up from the table, looked at him, still breathing heavily, and just said, "Oh my."

He just stood in front of me, smiling at me.

I ran my eyes up and down his body, appreciating his muscular features and then locked them on his penis, swaying in front of him, wet with a mixture of our juices. Acting purely on impulse and desire, I slipped off the table and down to my knees once more, leaning forward and tilting my head to work him into my mouth. I closed my eyes and just savored his penis in my mouth. I held still, feeling it pulse against my tongue, tasting the sweetness from my orgasm and his precum.

Unconsciously, I pushed my knees apart and let my hand

drop between my legs once more, feeling how wet he had me, and how easily two of my fingers slipped inside. I let his head slip from my lips and began running them up and down the shaft, stroking him with them, running my tongue over him, submissively worshiping his beautiful cock, showing him my appreciation for the pleasure he gave me.

He stepped back and took my hand, helping me to my feet, then led me into the bedroom. I slipped off my high heels and he laid me on my back in the middle of the bed. Starting at the bottom of the bed, he crawled up between my legs, dropped his head down and drove his tongue against me. He flicked his tongue across my clit and lapped at me for a few minutes before kissing his way up my stomach.

Once over my breasts, he began kissing them, sucking my nipples into his mouth, and teasing them with his teeth, then moving up to my lips. Holding himself over top of me, I ran my hands up and down his muscular forearms and biceps as he deeply kissed me, occasionally fucking my mouth with his tongue.

Breaking the kiss, he continued further forward on his knees, straddling my arms and breasts, he guided the head of his cock back into my mouth. Steadying himself with his hands on the headboard, he rolled his hips forward and began slowly stroking himself in and out of my lips. He stared down at me intensely, looking deep into my eyes as he rolled his hips forward, each time pushing a little further into my throat until his motion was nothing short of fucking my mouth. When he pulled out, my eyes were watering, and I was gasping and coughing as he quickly moved down my body and pushed my legs apart.

I felt him hook his forearm behind one of my knees and push it up to my shoulder, spreading my legs and opening my hips as he used his free hand to guide himself into me. Once inside, he held me in this position, thrusting his hips at a fevered pace. I could feel the full weight of his body coming down on me, almost knocking the wind out of me with every thrust. He was going at me harder than I'd ever been fucked before. A steady moan and grunts escaped my throat with each thrust as he pounded into me. I honestly started to wonder how much more of this I could handle, when he finally growled out loud.

With one final hard thrust into me, he quickly pulled out and moved up over my hips.

Through his ragged breath, he was saying, "I'm gonna

cum … Stroke it! Stroke it!"

Still recovering from his onslaught, I brought my hands up to take his shaft in my fingers and began pumping it. A loud moan escaped his lips as he arched his back and released. I continued pumping his hard shaft, feeling his cock pulsing in my hands and watching streams of white spray from the tip up over my stomach and breasts.

"UUUUUUGGGHHHHH," echoed through the room as I stared up at him, milking him over my breasts to get the last drops.

As he relaxed back, he pushed himself up from the bed and wandered off to the bathroom, leaving me lying there in my stockings and covered in his cum. A few seconds later, he returned with a towel, gently wiping me and telling me how incredible that was. After cleaning me up, he pulled the covers up over me and laid down behind me and we fell asleep.

I woke up about two A.M., and realized I needed to get back to my room. He was rolled over and snoring in quite a cute way. I quietly slipped out of bed, still wearing my stockings, garter belt, and panties, picked up my high heels, and crept out to the living room. I found my dress on the floor and slipped it on, then my heels, and made my way back to my room.

I looked at the mirrors in the elevator and realized how rough I looked, that just fucked look. Fortunately, I didn't run into anyone in the hallway. Back in my room, I stripped off all my clothes and jumped in for a quick rinse off before climbing in the bed naked to pass back out.

CHAPTER TWELVE

Day Two

After snoozing my alarm three times and telling myself the booth was just fine without me, I finally pried myself out of bed. I sat up on the edge, naked and chilled from the air conditioning, and I began feeling the remnants of the previous night.

I could feel a slight hangover and dull headache from drinking. My throat was a little scratchy and my jaw was actually sore. I was expecting to feel quite used between my legs, but surprisingly it wasn't that bad. Don't get me wrong, I could definitely tell how hard he fucked me, but it wasn't like I was going to be walking bow legged.

I got another quick shower, mostly just to wake me up, then did my hair and makeup. Walking over to my suitcases wrapped only in a towel, I began looking through my options to see what I felt like today. I chose a short sleeve, gray, button-up dress with black accents and buttons. The hem fell at mid-thigh, and I could always leave a button undone at the top or bottom if I wanted to make it a little flirtier. Underneath I wore my black sheer bra and a pair of black sheer-to-waist pantyhose, the same as the nude pair I wore the day before, without the cotton gusset and only the thin seam. My pair of black, closed toe, slingback high heels completed the outfit.

I was thinking ahead and knew I had another 20-minute presentation to give this afternoon, so I figured the black hose would give me a little more concealment. It wasn't that I didn't want to be playful and teasing, I just felt like two days in a row might look a little obvious.

It was almost ten A.M. when I finally made it to the booth, large coffee in hand and ready to sell. I was deliberately trying to put the previous night out of my mind as long as I could. There was a lot there for me to wrap my head around. What I did. What it was like. What happens now. I just needed to keep my head in the game and there was more than enough there to distract me.

Just getting settled in, I noticed there was a man in the booth next to mine, and not the woman that was there the previous day. He was a handsome older gentleman, distinguished in his looks.

"Hi, where's—Janet, was it?" I asked to be friendly.

He made his way over into my booth and introduced himself as Jack, the owner of the company. He went on to tell me that Janet had some other appointments she had to take care of today and would be back tomorrow for the last day. He then turned on the charm, saying, "Had I known I'd get to look at such a pretty lady like you all day, I would have done the entire show myself."

"Aww, thank you, you're too sweet."

Throughout the rest of the morning, Jack continued to flirt and stole a couple glances at my thighs as I climbed on and off my stool.

A little after noon, my phone went off, it was a text from Aaron.

```
Hello    beautiful!!!    I
wish  I  could  have  woken
up   beside   you...  you   at
```

your booth?

> Sorry, I had to get ready for the day. Yes, I'm down here now.

K, I have a bunch of meetings today, but I'll try to get down there to see you

> I'll be here till 4, then I have another 20 min presentation

K ;-)

Today was a little slower than the previous day, so Jack and I had time to talk as he kept making his way to my booth. He told me he was married, with his kids all grown and moved on, and how his wife and him kind of do their own things now. He asked about my situation but was very adamant in making sure I knew that he and his wife had grown apart. Eventually he worked up to asking me if I'd like to join him for drinks at the hotel bar after the show wrapped up today. I told him I would have loved to, but I already had plans to meet with someone else that evening. I wasn't lying, I would have gone and had drinks with him, but I was anticipating Aaron wanting to see me again.

Not that I'm exclusive with Aaron, I did just meet him, and I am married, but there's only one more evening at the show. I could tell Jack was disappointed, but he continued to flirt and watch me, and I took the liberty a few times to bend and squat down in his view, letting him see a little something.

Around three P.M., Aaron stopped by my booth, greeted me with a hug and a kiss, and complimented me on my performance the night before. He told me he was looking forward to seeing me again that evening if I was up for it, but he wasn't sure what time since he had some meetings to attend. Trying not to sound too eager, I told him I would love to see him again, and to just text me.

I went on to tease him, telling him, "My new friend next door, Jack, asked me to join him for drinks tonight, but I told him I was supposed to meet someone. I hope you don't stand me up, I might just have to call him."

"Hmmm, I have competition, do I?"

"Well, I don't know, I'm a pretty popular girl, all the guys

137

are asking me out," I teased back.

Aaron leaned over to look at Jack, then turned back to me, saying, "Seems like a nice enough guy, maybe he deserves a chance."

He smiled and turned, walking away and saying, "I'll text you."

No sooner did Aaron turn the corner of the aisle and Jack was headed back over to my booth.

"That your husband?"

A little taken off guard by his question, I stuttered, "Uhhh … No … He's… just a friend."

He gave me a wink and said, "Aaahh, I understand. It's like what happens in Vegas. What happens at the trade show stays at the trade show, right?"

A little embarrassed, I smiled and said, "Uhh, something like that I suppose."

Then he joked and said as he walked away, "Well, if you need another friend, I'm right over here."

I just rolled my eyes and shook my head, laughing as I turned to talk to some people walking up. The afternoon picked up a little bit and the time passed quickly. Before I knew it, I had to head over for my second 20-minute presentation.

I got into the room a little early, and as before, there was a young attractive saleswoman giving her pitch before me. And just like before, she was sitting in a short black skirt, with bare legs, and giving flashes of her black panties repeatedly. It was really nothing that bad, and her black panties hid everything, but I know for most men it's just the thought that they got a glimpse of something they weren't supposed to see.

I got up on stage, a little more confident this time, and breezed through my presentation. I know several of the men got a clear look up my dress, but with the black hose I'm sure they probably didn't even realize I wasn't wearing panties underneath.

While I walked back to the main hall to finish out the day, I received a text from Aaron.

```
Hey, sorry, I have to go
to dinner with some
associates and won't be
back until after 10… can
I see you then?
```

I was a little disappointed when I read his text but didn't

want it to sound that way.

```
                    That's fine, just text me
```

```
K
```

There was little pause, and then my phone beeped again.

```
now you can have those
drinks with Jack
```

```
                    haha, I was just saying that
                    to tease you, I wasn't really
                    going to
```

```
would you have if I
wasn't here?
```

```
                    yes, he's handsome ;-)
```

```
then you should do it… I
want you to do it
```

I don't get it … Why is he telling me to do it?

I didn't respond right away—I didn't know what to say,

then he texted again.

```
I'm   serious.  do   it.
tonight I want to hear
about it... I want to hear
about what you did with
him... I dare you ;-)
```

```
            You're joking, right?
```

```
no... I'm serious. you
told me you would do what
I  wanted... I'm telling
you  to  go  have  drinks
with him and if he wants
more... I want you to do it
```

I can't believe he's telling me that.

```
            Really? You want me to do
            something with him?
```

```
YES... tell me you will... it
will drive me crazy all
night thinking about it...
promise me
```

This is crazy.

I was so surprised at what he was asking that I didn't text right back, and he messaged again.

```
promise me
```

I can't believe I'm going to do this.

```
                    Alright, I promise
```

```
good... I want to hear all
about it tonight
```

As I walked into the exhibit hall, I was thinking back on the night before. What Aaron had me do in front of the driver, then in front of the men in the elevator, it excites him to have that influence over me and involve other people. That's why he wants me to do this, because he told me to. When I returned to my booth, I thought perhaps it wasn't going to work out since Jack was nowhere to be seen.

He must be gone for the day.

Just then, I heard a voice from behind me say, "I thought

you left me," and turned to see Jack walking toward me.

"No, I just had to go give a short presentation."

I took a deep breath and then continued, "And actually, my plans for the evening got pushed back, so I'm free until nine if you still wanted to grab that drink."

His eyes lit up and I could tell he was genuinely excited; little did he know what was already decided for him. He stepped forward and gave me a quick hug, saying, "I'm so glad, I'm ready whenever you are."

It was just after five, and things had started to slow so I cheerfully agreed, "Yeah, let's get out of here—I could use a drink."

We left the hall and walked through the hotel to the lobby bar. I could tell agreeing to go have a drink with him boosted his confidence that I was responding to his advances, because as we walked, he had his hand on my lower back and would drop it down to brush the top of my ass through my dress. When I didn't say or do anything to object, he would drop it a little further. By the time we were standing in the short line to enter the bar, his hand was resting on the outside curve of my ass, gently caressing. I just continued our conversation, laughing at his jokes and engaging. He really was funny and pleasant to talk to.

The back wall of the bar had a plush bench seat that extended the entire length with small round tables spaced out along it. A couple stood up and left just as we walked through so we had a seat. Almost immediately the waitress stopped by. I ordered rum and Coke and Jack ordered a beer, but then added two shots of tequila, chilled.

As the waitress walked away, I looked over at him and commented, "Who are those for?"

He smiled at me and said, "I figured we should kick off our friendship with a toast, and me and my buddies always toast with tequila."

Let's see—coffee for breakfast, a bagel at lunch, and now tequila—yeah, this isn't going to be good.

"Alright, I'll do one toast," but after a short pause, I joked, "You're not trying to get me drunk, are you?"

"Whatever would make you think that?" he responded, shaking his head and laughing.

We continued with small talk, but laden with sexual innuendos.

As pleasant as he was, Jack was more of what I was accustomed to at trade shows. There was no doubt that his entire intention was to see how far he could get with me in the time we had. And since I gave him a deadline of nine o'clock, he's clearly trying to accelerate the process.

The waitress set our drinks down and Jack handed her cash, then picked up the tequila and raised his glass toward me.

The first thing that went through my mind was, *that's not a shot of tequila, that's a glass of tequila.*

Raising the glass to him, I couldn't help but comment, "That's a lot of tequila, I don't know if I can do all that."

He clinked his glass with mine and encouraged me, "It doesn't have to be all in one shot, I'm sure we can make several toasts. So, the first toast, to you, my new beautiful friend."

I just smiled as we took our first shot. I did a pretty good bit, and my glass was still half full.

Wow! Definitely not top shelf, I thought as I felt the burn go down my throat.

I picked up my mixed drink to chase the shot and as I brought it to my lips, Jack slipped his hand on my knee under the table. I was sitting, turned slightly towards him with my legs together but not crossed, holding my drink with my right hand, my left elbow up on the back of the bench seat with my hand resting on the back of my head, running my fingers through my hair. My body language indicated I was relaxed and open to his advances.

Over the next twenty minutes or so, we shared some stories, did the second shot, this time toasting to getting to know each other better, and his hand worked its way to the middle of my thigh, testing the hem of my dress. A few minutes after the second shot, I felt a warm wave go through my body as the alcohol really began to hit me. Jack noticed as well, asking if I was okay. I just laughed, making a short blowing motion with my lips, "Whew ... Yes, I'm good —just felt that alcohol start to hit me. Have to say it does feel nice to be relaxed."

The eager sexual anticipation was written all over his face in response to my comment about feeling it. I was starting to get giggly, laughing at everything he said as he raised his glass one last time to do the final shot.

Okay, last one ...

Jack was definitely feeling his drinks just as much as I. After he made the final toast, he removed any doubt of his intentions or where we were headed. As my head was tipped back, downing the last of the tequila, my knees relaxed open,

146

and he slid his hand all the way up the inside of my thigh under the short bottom of my dress. His fingers were squeezing the soft skin of my thigh through my pantyhose and his pinky was brushing back and forth over the lips of my pussy through the nylon.

I didn't say anything. I just set my glass down and looked over at him as he intently stared at me and continued to move his fingers against me. I picked up my rum and Coke and finished the last of it, then looked back at him licking my lips, slowly blinking my eyes and feeling my drunkenness growing by the second.

He broke the silence, asking, "You feel like you need to lie down? Why don't we go up to your room?"

"Yeah, that's probably a good idea."

I was getting drunker by the minute as the drinks I had were hitting my bloodstream, but I still was aware of the game we were playing. The only difference now was that my inhibitions were gone. Jack stood up and stepped around the small table, helping me to my feet. I was a little wobbly on my high heels, so he put his arm around my waist to steady me as we walked out. I noticed a few looks on people's faces in the room, knowing where we were going and what I was about to do.

The lobby was busy, and the elevator was full of people as we made our way to my floor, me giggling and swaying as Jack took every opportunity to grope me. Stumbling down the hallway, I started to wonder if we would even make it to the room as his hands were all over me and he kissed me a few times. I finally got my door open as he stood behind me, holding my hips and grinding himself against me. As soon as the door to the room shut, he had me against the wall, kissing me and unbuttoning the front of my dress.

My eyes were closed, and everything was surreal as I felt his hands moving over my body, slipping my dress down off my shoulders, then pushing my bra down. His hands and mouth were working over my breasts, sucking on my nipples and squeezing them. He continued sucking on my right breast, teasing my nipple in his mouth with his teeth as he dropped his right hand down between my legs and began to rub me through my hose. My head was back against the wall with my eyes closed, moans escaping my lips as he stimulated my nipples.

I could feel his fingers working between my legs, then heard a ripping sound as he tore a hole in the crotch of my

148

pantyhose to push his fingers into me. I let out a gasp as he pushed one finger, then quickly followed by a second, up into me and pumping them in and out. Standing back up, he began to kiss me again, still working his fingers between my legs.

He slid his hand away then led me over to the bed, laying me down on my back and spinning me so my head was at the bottom of the bed, hanging back. I laid there, running my fingertips over my breasts and looking up at him as he unbuckled his pants and took them off.

Sliding his boxers down, his erection sprung free. He was average size, maybe five inches or so with dark brown pubic hair, neatly trimmed. As he continued to unbutton his shirt, he stepped forward and spread his feet, lowering his hips to guide the head of his penis to my lips. As the tip touched, I opened my mouth and let him slide in, continuing to push forward until he was all the way into my mouth. Since he was nowhere near the size of Aaron, I was easily able to accommodate his full strokes as he rocked his hips back and forth.

Feeling the full effects of the alcohol now, I mostly just laid there letting him use my mouth, occasionally reaching up to stroke him or run my fingernails across his balls. He was rocking his hips back and forth, sliding in and out of my lips as he fondled my breasts and slid a hand down between my legs to finger me through the hole in my pantyhose. He was starting to get really hard and frenzied as he stepped back, took hold of my arms and helped spin me around, turning me on to my stomach and laying over the bottom edge of the bed.

My hips were at the edge and my legs were extended back to the floor, still wearing my black sheer pantyhose and high heels. I could feel him stepping up to straddle the back of my thighs, then felt him rip the hole in my pantyhose a little larger. He lowered himself down, rubbing the head of his penis up and down the lips of my pussy a few times before pushing forward to penetrate me. I was so relaxed into the bed, letting out a low steady moan as I felt the weight of his hips coming down against the sheer nylon still covering the cheeks of my ass.

His hands were on the backs of my forearms, holding my arms at my sides as he started talking to me, saying, "You feel so good … You're sooo beautiful."

I could hear the slur in his speech as well.

He fucked me in this position for a few more minutes, then stepped back, telling me to climb up on the bed. I slowly pushed myself up and crawled forward to the middle of the bed, falling back down onto my stomach. He climbed back on top of me from behind, sliding back into me for another minute or so. He just kept saying over and over how beautiful I was and how good I felt.

Then he slowed down and got up on his knees, saying, "I wanna do somethin' ... I wanna do somethin' to you. Can I do somethin' to you?"

We were both drunk and he wasn't making sense to me, but I just mumbled, "Yeah ... Do whatever you want—it all feelz good."

I could feel him rocking slightly on the back of my thighs, then his hands moved over my ass and squeezed my cheeks. But then I felt the head of his penis. He was rubbing it up and down the crack of my ass, moving it over my opening.

That's what he meant   that's what he wanted ...

In my drunken state, I was relaxed and not caring, so I let out a little moan and then just said, "Jus go slow."

I'd only had anal sex a few times in my life, with mostly good experiences, but experimented many times while masturbating, so it was arousing to let him take me that way. In my mind, letting a man do that is such a submissive and intimate act, and I found it incredibly erotic, especially in this situation with this man I barely knew.

I felt the pressure from the head of his penis as he began to push his hips forward. Thanks to the alcohol, I was already relaxed and a little bit numb to everything. He continued slowly pushing forward, increasing the pressure against my opening, until finally the head slipped inside.

"Uuuuhhhh," escaped my throat, muffled into the bed as I felt him enter me and slowly push deeper.

I curled my fingers into the bedspread, gripping it tightly as he slowly rocked back and forth, inching his way deeper into me. He finally worked every inch all the way into my ass as he laid forward, lowering his body down on top of mine. His hands worked up under my body, placing his palms under each of my breasts to squeeze them as he began rolling his hips, gyrating himself into me. My breathing was shallow, trying to stay relaxed and feeling the weight of his body pinning me to the bed as he impaled me. Still gripping the comforter, low grunts and a steady moan escaped my lips as he began thrusting his hips more intently.

I could hear his breathing right at my ear, moaning as he said to me, "Oh my God … Your ass feelz so good! My wife won't let me do this … Oh my God."

What little discomfort I felt was now gone and while I felt incredibly full, it was starting to feel good for me as well. When my moans transitioned to a more pleasurable tone, it clearly aroused him—and he started thrusting faster.

"Does that feel good? You like it?" he asked through his heavy breathing.

I knew what he wanted to hear as I slurred. "Yeah … Yeah … It feelz good."

"Tell me where … Tell me where I'm fucking you," he demanded with an urgency in his slurred words.

"Uuuugghhh … My ass … Ughh … You're fucking my ass," I uttered back through my moans.

The more I moaned, the faster and harder he would thrust, and the more I would moan. This cycle escalated until he was slamming his hips down against my ass, causing me to cry out with every thrust.

His feet were hooked inside my ankles now and he had my legs spread open wide as he pumped his hips into me for the next few minutes. If not for the alcohol, I'm sure he would not have lasted this long by how excited he was, nor would I have probably been able to endure his pounding into me in

153

this spread-eagled position. He finally drove himself deep into me one last time, squeezing my breasts tight with his fingers. I felt when he began to release and his body quivered on top of mine, pinning me to the bed. A loud groan escaped his throat right beside my ear as he pulsed his hips and released everything he had into me. After he laid on top of me for a moment, he slowly rolled off to the side.

He was repeatedly slurring, "Thank you … Thank you for that."

I didn't even verbally answer as I just let out a low sigh and moan. I remember the bed moving a little as he got up and then I must have fallen asleep.

CHAPTER THIRTEEN

10 P.M., Time to Wake Up

What ... What is that? What the ...

I woke up disoriented, to my phone beeping and ringing repeatedly and a knocking at my hotel room door. I pushed myself up from the bed, naked except for my pantyhose and high heels that I still had on and made my way over to the hallway where my phone was lying on the floor. I picked it up and saw missed calls and messages from Aaron's number, then a loud knock at the door startled me as I was standing right beside it. Leaning forward, I peeked through the hole to see Aaron in the hallway. Taking a deep breath and trying not to be as drunk as I still was, I slowly opened the door, not even giving thought to the fact that I was practically naked.

As soon as Aaron saw me, a big smile came across his face and he said, "Well, it looks like you've had a fun evening so far. Does this mean you had drinks with Jack after all?"

"Oh my God, yes, we had drinks," and I laughed as I shook my head.

Everything that happened just a short time ago in my room was a little bit of a blur as I tried to piece it together. Aaron stepped into the room, his hand going straight to my breasts and the other dropping to squeeze my ass.

"So, I'm guessing you have a lot to tell me," he said as he turned my body slightly to the side to look down at the hole in the back of my pantyhose.

"Yes, I do. Let me change and I'll tell you."

"No, keep this on—I want you just the way you were with him, telling me what he did with you."

He led me by the hand over to the bed. He was amused at how unsteady I still was in my high heels, commenting, "You're really drunk, aren't you?"

"Oh my God, he got us these tequila shots, but it was like

a glass of tequila, an he kep making up toasts, an I hadn't really eaten all day, an I had a rum and Coke, and … it was jus' too much for me," I rambled with a slur.

I could tell he was amused at my state as he said "Alright, alright, come over here and tell me all about it—while you go down on me."

I stood in front of him, swaying back and forth as I watched him quickly strip out of his clothes and climb into the middle of the bed to lay on his back.

He spread his legs wide, his penis semi-erect laying against his thigh as he looked up at me and said, "Come on, lay down here and kiss me while you tell me everything."

I climbed onto the bed and laid down on my side, against his thigh, taking his penis into my hand and lowering my lips down to lightly kiss the soft head. He let out a relaxing sigh as I slipped my lips over the head and began sucking and stroking him to life. Once I had him hard and my saliva lubricating the shaft, I lifted my head up and began telling him the events of the evening as I slowly stroked my fingers up and down the length of him.

I told him how things started in the bar, his hand on my leg and moving under my dress and groping me all the way up the elevator to my room. Dropping my head down, I took him back into my mouth for a moment, tasting the sweet pre-cum that was beginning to seep from the tip.

I continued my recollection, describing the way he undressed me inside my room, kissing my breasts, and ripping my pantyhose to push his fingers into me. Aaron especially enjoyed the part where Jack laid me on the bed with my head hung back and slid into my mouth while he ran his hands over my body. I could tell all this excited him by how hard he was, but also the slippery precum that was flowing from the tip of his penis.

I detailed how he spun me around and bent me over the bottom of the bed, straddling me to fuck me as he pinned my arms down. Again, I paused my story as I took him back into my mouth, moving my hands to his thighs as I bobbed my head, taking him as deep as I comfortably could in that position.

I heard the arousal in Aaron's voice as he asked, "Is that it? Is that how he was fucking you when he came?"

Bringing my hand back to his shaft, I began stroking him again as I lifted my head and said, "No, there's one more thing he did to me."

I could see the anticipation in Aaron's eyes as he said, "Tell me."

"He had me get up on the bed and lay on my stomach, then he climbed up on top of me and started to fuck me again, but then he stopped."

"Go on."

"He asked me if he could do somethin' to me, but I didn't know what he meant, and I was drunk and I said, 'Yes, whatever you want'."

Aaron was so excited and breathing shallow as he asked, "What did he want? What did he do to you?"

I dropped my lips around his head again as a quick tease, then looked up and said, "He started sliding his cock between the cheeks of my ass, and then he pushed into me—he pushed into my ass."

"Oh my God! He fucked your ass? You let him do that to you? Do you like that?"

I gave a little embarrassed laugh as I slowly continued to stroke him, answering, "Yeah, I let him do it—I told him to go slow, but by the time he came, he was ramming into me."

"Did you like it? Did you like him fucking your ass?"

Aaron was so excited asking me that his body was

trembling as he intensely stared at me, waiting for my answer. I felt a little embarrassed as I quietly said, "Yeah, I liked it," then quickly dropped my mouth back down around his shaft to suck him deep into my mouth.

So intensely aroused by my answer, Aaron's hands came to the back of my head and began pushing me down on him, thrusting his hips up, causing me to gag a couple times. When he released my hair, I raised my head up and caught my breath, looking up to see how incredibly aroused he became at hearing what I did. Staring down into my eyes, I could see he was thinking about something, trying to decide what he wanted.

"I want you to fuck me," finally escaped his lips, followed by, "First, climb on top of me."

I pushed myself up to my hands and knees and crawled up over his body, straddling his hips. My ripped black pantyhose, open to expose my pussy, hovered over top of the head of his penis. Lowering myself down, a moan escaped my throat as I felt him penetrate me, pleasantly appreciating his size. Once my hips were settled all the way down onto him, I brought my feet in, still wearing my black high heels, and hooked the toes inside his thighs as I began to roll my hips,

160

my hands steadying myself on his chest.

He just laid back, watching me as I pleasured myself on him, my breasts bouncing and swaying with my movements. He let me do this until an orgasm rippled through my body. I was fully impaled on his stiff shaft, my body trembling and convulsing as I brought one hand up to squeeze my breasts.

After my orgasm subsided, I opened my eyes and looked down to see him intensely staring up at me, and then saying, "Now it's my turn—you're gonna make me cum."

In my somber state, I submissively said, "Anything you want."

A little smile formed on his lips as he said, "Mmmm, that's right—stand up."

I pushed myself off of him and moved over to the edge of the bed to step off. Aaron sat up and slid down to the bottom, sitting on the edge and telling me to walk over in front of him. I lowered myself to my knees and took him into my mouth, tasting my sweetness and assuming he wanted me to suck him off. He let me go for a minute, doing my best to pump him into my mouth and make him cum, but that's not what he wanted.

"Stand up."

Pushing myself back to my feet, I stood in front of him, my arms to my sides, my feet shoulder width, swaying my hips in front of him, a little uncertain of what he wanted me to do. He laid back onto the bed, propped up on his elbows, his feet and knees spread open wide, and his hips pushed forward as he said, "Turn around and sit on me—make me cum."

Still feeling my alcohol, I looked down at him, teasingly biting my lip and swaying a sultry way as I spun my back to him and moved into position. Seductively peeking back over my shoulder at him, I brought my high heels together, put my hands on his knees to steady myself, and sat down over his erection. I felt the head of his cock begin to press against the lips of my pussy as I wiggled my hips a little, lining him up and slowly letting him enter me.

I only had an inch or so in when I heard him say, "Not there. Give me what you gave Jack—make me cum with your ass.

Immediately I thought to myself, *Oh my God! There's no way … He's too big … I can't handle that …*

I held my position and looked back at him, nervously saying, "I don't know if I can—you're so big."

He was looking at me with an intense stare and said, "You can do it—just go slow."

Wishing I had another shot of tequila right then, I pushed up with my legs, slipping him out of my pussy and reaching back with my right hand to take the shaft and guide him to the opening of my ass. Trying to relax my breathing, I held him for a few seconds as I let the weight of my body lower my hips against him. I could feel the tip beginning to open me as I moved my hand back to his knee to steady myself, lowering down as gently as possible. I could feel my body trembling as I blew relaxing breaths in and out of my lips, letting out a loud groan when the head finally slipped inside of me.

This was an entirely different experience, one that I'd never had before. Every time I'd done this with a man, he was on top of me or behind me, and I was at his mercy. I was the one in control here, I was the one impaling myself on this massive penis. I held still for a few seconds, trying to relax and adjust to his size before slowly flexing my thighs and beginning a pulsing movement.

Through my deep breaths and intense trembling, I heard Aaron's voice say, "God, you're so tight—that feels so good … Now fuck me."

Not wanting to disappoint, and determined to give him what he wanted, I began flexing my thighs again, letting myself drop a little deeper each time. I felt like I was in a Lamaze class, trying to control my breathing and moaning out loud as I began a slow, but steady bounce on him. It felt like I was completely impaling myself on his shaft, but I reached back with my hand to feel him as I moved up and down.

Oh Jesus ... That's only half of him ... There's no way I can take all of it.

I continued to bounce on him, my thighs beginning to burn from supporting myself and not going all the way down—but there was no way.

Again, Aaron's voice cut through, but now more anxious and labored, "That's it baby, keep fucking me ... Come on, fuck me harder ... Faster ... Make me explode."

My moaning transitioned into crying out as I intensified my motion, taking him even deeper. At one point, I pushed all the way up off him, needing to stand for a second as my legs were beginning to give out. I looked back at him, the expression on my face telling him how intense this was for me, and he just pleaded, "Just a little more—I'm so close—you're gonna make me cum."

I took a deep breath and nodded to him, affirming I could do it as I stepped back between his legs and lowered myself back down. Now feeling more relaxed and accustomed to his size, once I had the tip inside of me, I was able to slide down onto him easier. It still made my body tremble and evoked deep groans from my throat, but I began bouncing more vigorously on him, trying to make him explode as quickly as I could.

I could hear him moaning and saying things incoherent, telling me he was getting close to his orgasm. I felt his large hands slide up and close around the outside of my hips, just holding me as I continued my movement.

He started moaning out, "Oh yeah, oh yeah … I'm gonna cum … I'm gonna cum."

His fingers tightly gripped the outside of my hips over the sheer nylon of my pantyhose when he let out a loud cry, at the same time, pulling down on my hips, driving himself even deeper into my ass.

"Uuuuuuuugghhhhhhh," echoed through the room from my throat as my body shook. He was holding me tight down on him as he pulsed his hips up and released inside of me.

After at least twenty seconds or so, he finally relaxed his

grip, and I was able to push myself up to my feet. I stumbled forward, my legs weak and trembling as I steadied myself in my high heels against the dresser. Still breathing in a labored fashion, my body was trembling but beginning to relax from the deep penetration I just experienced.

Aaron was sitting up at the bottom of the bed, recovering from his orgasm as he looked up at me with a huge smile on his face and telling me, "That was amazing!"

While my experience was a little different than his, I will agree it was incredibly intense and like nothing I'd ever felt. While it wasn't the same pleasure that he felt, I did feel a sense of emotional excitement and it was hot getting him so aroused and making him cum that way.

Aaron got dressed and told me again how thankful he was and amazed with me, which only served to flatter me and stroke my ego. We both knew the conference was over the next day and this would be our last evening, but he assured me he would see me through the day before he left. I said goodnight and went into the bathroom to take a nice hot bath before heading to bed.

He was sitting in the chair putting his shoes on and before I closed the door to the bathroom, he asked if I had to give another presentation on stage tomorrow. I told him I did—around two-thirty—and he said he'd try to make it.

I closed the door, kicked off my heels, took off my ripped pantyhose, and began running a bath. A few minutes later I heard him let himself out.

CHAPTER FOURTEEN

Day Three

Since the night before with Aaron finished up by midnight, I felt like I had a full night's sleep and was surprisingly rested when I woke up. I sat up in bed, propping myself on my extended arms and just thought for a moment, flashing through everything that happened.

What am I doing? This has been quite a trip, I thought to myself, shaking my head in disbelief at my actions.

I made my way into the bathroom, and after the first few steps I was reminded of what I did with my bum the night before as I felt a little sore. I got a quick rinse off in the shower, did my hair and makeup, then packed up my toiletries. I had a late check out, but I figured I'd just take everything with me now and be done. I walked over to my two suitcases, stooped down, wrapped in my towel, and I began organizing things and pulling out what I was going to wear for the day.

What the heck? Where … Where are my underwear?

I was confused, questioning my sanity, as I dug through my suitcases and couldn't find a single pair of panties or a bra. Then I noticed there were no pantyhose either. The only things there, aside from my dresses, were thigh-highs, stockings, and my two garter belts. I sat for a moment trying to think what could have happened to them, then started thinking about Jack being in my room after I fell asleep.

Did he take my underwear? Is he one of those guys? I know guys used to do that kind of thing in college—but maybe? Ugh!

Coming to the realization there was nothing I could do about it right now, I pulled out the dress I was planning to wear today—a short, sleeveless, purple wrap dress with ties at the hips. I realized I did still have the black pantyhose from the day before, but they weren't an option since the crotch was completely torn open and they had a few remnants from my encounters on them. I threw them in the garbage, and pulled out a pair of black, sheer, stay-up thigh-highs.

After getting everything packed up, I sat down on the edge of the bed and slid my nylons up my legs, wrapped my dress around my naked body and tied it at the hips. Stepping into my four-inch black high heels with a D'Orsay cut, I made a final check in the mirror. The material of my dress was very thin and silky, which amplified the feeling of nakedness without my bra or panties. While the material was opaque enough, you could clearly see my nipples imprinted on the front and tell that I wasn't wearing a bra the way my breasts would move under the material.

Getting on the elevator with my luggage, a gentleman was nice enough to help me and was immediately rewarded with a view of most of my right breast as the top of my dress relaxed open when I leaned forward to move my bag.

I made it all the way to my booth with my bags and tucked them under the skirting of one of the tables. As I stooped down pushing the bags under, I noticed the lace top of my thigh-high revealed where my dress parted open, and I realized that every single thing I did today was going to expose me somehow. This dress was a little short for thigh-high nylons and not having underwear on made me feel arousingly self-conscious around so many people.

Looking over at the booth beside me, I saw that Janet was back.

I assume I'm never going to see Jack again—probably for the best since he stole my underwear.

Around eleven o'clock, I just finished giving a pitch to three men from a warehouse facility—who had zero interest in my products—but just wanted to get close and ogle me. They walked away, continuing to look back and enjoy the effect of my nipples under the thin material, clearly talking about me, when I saw Aaron approaching.

Greeting me with a large smile, a warm hug, and soft kiss on the lips, he started the conversation by reiterating how much he enjoyed the night before. I agreed, telling him it was quite intense and memorable for me as well. Then I started to share with him, "You're never going to believe this! Jack, the guy that was in my room before you got there, I think he stole all my underwear. I passed out when we were done and I don't remember him leaving, so it had to be—"

I stopped in mid-sentence as Aaron began laughing hysterically, then reached into his coat pocket and pulled out a receipt and handed it to me.

"What are you laughing at? What's this?"

I gave him a puzzled look and then I looked at the receipt. It was from FedEx.

"What is this?" I asked again.

Still laughing, he said, "That's the tracking number for your underwear. I took them after you went into the bathroom, and I shipped them back to your office this morning."

My mouth dropped open, and I playfully smacked him in the arm, asking, "Why did you do that, I don't have any other underwear with me. I'm standing here naked under my dress, and I have to give a presentation on stage this afternoon!"

Still laughing, he replied, "I know—that's what gave me the idea to take them all. I thought it'd be fun to see you one last time, sitting up there in the bright lights, all nervous, and then exposing yourself to all of us," he teased.

"Don't worry, I plan on being front and center for that presentation."

"Oh my God, you are so bad!"

"I don't know, I thought it was pretty clever of me."

"What time is your flight this evening?" he continued, trying to change the subject.

"I have to be at the airport by six-thirty."

"Alright, I have a car coming to pick me up later, so I can give you a ride and drop you off. I have to run right now, but I'll see you at your presentation—all of you!" he said with another laugh and walked off.

I can't believe he did that …

The next couple hours went by quickly, with a steady stream of people coming through, mostly men, and mostly wanting to just get a look at me. I was feeling much more playful and sexier, starting to feel a little excited about the last presentation I was going to give.

Flirting with most of the men that stopped by my booth, I would touch their arm or give them a playful hug when laughing at a joke, pressing my breasts against them. I even loosened the ties on my wrap dress slightly, letting the material fall a little more freely, revealing the inner curve of my breast. Pretty sure I let one of my nipples peek out several times as I leaned over one of the tables to pick up a brochure.

It wasn't something I even intended to do, but one lucky guy actually got several seconds looking right up between my thighs and seeing all of me. A stack of brochures got knocked off the table and he stooped down in front of me to help as I was picking them up. I didn't even realize it at first honestly, then I looked up to thank him for his help and saw he was staring right at my legs. When I looked down at my thighs, the top wrap of my dress was stretched across my thighs and the way my feet were parted when I stooped down, my knees were several inches apart. Under the bright lights of the convention hall, I know he was staring right at the smooth lips of my exposed pussy. I felt an immediate rush of embarrassment go through my body but held myself there as I finished picking up all the brochures, letting him just look at me. I was thinking to myself, *In thirty minutes, I'm going to be exposed this way to a room full of men ... Might as well start with one now ...*

It was almost time for my presentation as I headed to the small room. I walked in as the woman on stage was finishing up. To the disappointment of all the men I'm sure, she was wearing black slacks and a white blouse. I stood there, getting ready to head to the stage when I felt hands grip my shoulders and heard Aaron's voice whispering in my ear, "Last day ... Look at all those men sitting there ... waiting for you to take the stage ... Ya know, you're never going to see these guys again—so ... give us a nice show—and I don't mean a quick flash at the end. I want to see you several times throughout your presentation—I want everyone to see you. Understand?"

He reached down and gave my butt a squeeze through my dress as I just shook my head, and with a nervous tremble in my voice, I answered, "We'll see."

"Noooo—not 'we'll see'," he playfully whispered back in my ear, "I want you tell me that you understand—tell me you understand that every guy here, sitting in front of you, looking up at you on that stage—you're going to look at all their faces ... look them in the eyes ... part your legs, and let them see your beautiful pussy—tell me."

Oh ... My ... God ... He's killing me! I thought, my nervousness now off the chart.

He knew exactly what he was doing, making sure I was completely present in the moment and hyper-focused on the submissive emotional rush I was about to experience. This was the opposite of a pep talk—this was pointing out all the obvious to make sure I felt every ounce of erotic embarrassment that he knew terrified me but made me so excited.

With another squeeze at my shoulders, he demanded again at my ear, "Tell me ..."

I was now physically trembling with nervousness, my breathing shallow and ragged, a knot in my stomach, and a lump in my throat as my eyes scanned the room of men, committing myself to my intimate performance, "I ... I understand."

"Good girl," was his only response before walking away to get a seat.

It seemed like with each step towards the stage, the closer I got, the more nervous I became. As I stepped up onto the stage, I looked out and saw the men filing into the seats, Aaron front and center as he said he would be. My legs were unsteady, and I could feel their eyes on me—I was so nervous.

The first day when I was exposed, I had pantyhose on, so it didn't really come across as being that bad, it was just a lucky view everyone got. But today, I'm wearing black thigh-highs, and there will be no missing the contrast against the skin of my thighs and my nakedness. The men that see me are going to believe—going to know—that I did this on purpose and wanted them all to see me. Why else would a woman put herself on stage in a short dress with thigh-highs and no panties? The only women I can think of that do that are strippers.

Confessions of a Saleswoman

I spoke briefly with the MC like before, but this was a different man. He looked me up and down and smiled, as if to say "Yeah, they're gonna like you."

Ushering me over to my seat, he stepped forward and began addressing the audience. I set my phone and papers down on the table, and turned, looking out at all the men listening to the MC but staring at me, and sat down.

Here goes ... Last time I'm here ... Never going to see any of these men again, I kept repeating in my mind.

And as the MC introduced me, I looked out at the faces, smiling, and crossed my legs. All eyes were on my legs as I made my first exposing move. I looked immediately at Aaron's face, and he just smiled and nodded, confirming what was revealed. I tried to focus on what I was saying and not think about what everyone was seeing as I continued through my presentation.

I crossed and uncrossed my legs at least five or six times, and in between, I sat with my knees relaxed in Aaron's direction, giving him, and ten other men, the perfect angle between my thighs. Finishing up, I felt like the applause was more for my display and showing their appreciation for what I just did. After I finished speaking, I handed the mic back to the MC and he made a few announcements.

Okay … Last time … Here you go guys …

As he spoke, I gathered my papers and then pretended to be distracted as I looked at my phone. I slid my hips forward to the very edge of the seat, the wrap of my dress parting off my legs slightly as I did, just beginning to reveal the lace of my thigh-highs. Then, as I scrolled on my phone, I acted totally oblivious as I shifted my feet apart and let my knees open, giving an undeniable full view of my nakedness to the room. I was physically shaking from the humiliating arousal I was experiencing doing this. It was a rush.

Finally picking up my papers, I pushed myself to my feet and, not making eye contact with anyone in the room, I hurried down off the stage and over to the side. I stood off to the side, still pretending to look at my phone as Aaron walked over to me. I looked up at him, giving a nervous laugh and saying, "I can't believe I just did that. Could you see? Could you see anything?"

He just shook his head, smiling back at me, and said, "Could I see anything? No, I could see everything! The guy beside me was like, 'Holy shit, do you see that?!', and I could hear little comments from a lot of the men all around me. You just flashed the whole room."

I looked out over Aaron's shoulder at the men still lingering in the room, and they were clearly watching in my direction. Some of them were pointing and nodding, but they were all smiling and sharing what they just witnessed.

I looked back at Aaron, "I'm so embarrassed!"

He couldn't stop smiling as he said, "Don't be—you made the day of every guy in this room. They'll remember that forever, and I guarantee some of them will remember it tonight when they're lying in bed," he joked.

"I feel like I need you to walk with me back to my booth, I don't want to get abducted out in the hall."

As we started to walk out, all the men were watching me, and Aaron joked, "What makes you think you're safe with me? Maybe I'm the one you have to worry about."

We walked down the hallway, and through the lobby. I continued to nervously go on about what I just did when I felt Aaron grab my arm and pull me quickly through a doorway by the elevators.

We were in the concrete stairwell next to the elevators.

"What are you doing?" I asked.

He led me back around the corner of the steps where we

were just out of view of the door, turned me to face the wall and stepped behind me, saying in my ear, "I told you — maybe I'm the one you have to worry about."

I heard the zipper to his pants go down and then felt his hand moving behind me before he raised the back of my dress. I spread my feet, arched my back slightly to push my butt out, then waited in anticipation as I felt him stroking his cock against my leg and then sliding it between my thighs. I was already wet and aroused from the events of the entire day, so he smoothly slid into my pussy and began pumping himself in and out of me right there against the wall. He reached around my shoulder and slid his hand into the top of my dress, fondling my breast and squeezing my nipple hard as he gave several deep thrusts into me, causing me to cry out. It felt wonderful — so raw and intense — especially with the state of mind I was in after just exposing myself so openly.

Suddenly, we heard a door open a few floors above us, and then footsteps and voices making their way down. Aaron brought his hand up and put it over my mouth, then gave a flurry of hard thrusts into me before pulling out and putting himself away. I smoothed the back of my dress down as he grabbed my wrist and we ran back out the door, laughing like two teenagers.

Walking back out into the lobby, I felt like everyone looking in our direction knew what we were doing, but obviously they didn't.

Once back at my booth, Aaron stayed for a few minutes, talking with me and taking a few opportunities to slide his hand under my dress again to tease me. Looking at his phone, he said reluctantly that he had to go, but would be back later to give me that ride to the airport.

CHAPTER FIFTEEN

Working Girl

After my whirlwind of three sexually charged days, my mind was everywhere but on work. I went through the motions, talking with people about our products, but honestly, I became the one flirting and steering the conversations to innuendos and tongue-in-cheek jokes. After spending the entire day in such a public setting with so little clothing covering my body, and then the exposure during my presentation, and Aaron taking me in the stairwell, I was as sexually charged as I could be. Plain and simple, I was horny!

I was actually desiring some of the men passing through my booth to touch me, wanting them to try to brush their hand across my ass or put their arm around me and feel their fingers move up my ribs to the outside curve of my breast, but none did.

It was finally time for me to leave. The booth would get broken down the next day and shipped back to our offices. My trip to *FABTEK* was going to be lucrative for the company, but for me it would be one of the most memorable three days of my life. Never have I, nor did I imagine, I would experience or do some of the things I did at the direction of a man I just met over the past three days.

Not wanting to pass up the last opportunity, I waited for two handsome guys to make their way from the end of the aisle and be right across from my booth before I stooped down, knees pointed in their direction, to pull my luggage from under the table. They weren't paying attention at first, so I just stayed there, stalling until I knew they saw me, but once they did, they couldn't look away. Making it much harder on myself than it actually was, I leaned over and reached back for the second suitcase, opening my knees wide, pushing one of my high heels out, straightening my leg, and flashing them my entire world.

I wasn't watching them directly for a few seconds as I

feigned struggle with the suitcase and was startled when I heard a voice right above me saying, "Do you need help with those?"

They were both standing right there over me, looking down, and right up my dress as I looked up and smiled, "Oh, you startled me—yeah—this bag seems to be stuck."

I continued to hold my position, pulling on the bag as both of them knelt down right in front of me, barely trying to hide that they were staring right between my thighs. The one guy even leaned forward to reach under the table and help with the bag, putting his head right in front of my knees.

Both of them were so focused on my legs, I don't think they even noticed that the top of my dress was pulled open as I reached over, barely covering my nipple. I was getting such a thrill out of this; I really had become quite an exhibitionist during this trip.

With his help, I was able to pull the bag from under the table and then slid my foot in as I turned toward them, but still letting my knees stay several inches apart. I continued to hold my squatted position for a few more seconds, smiling and thanking them for their help, before standing back up.

They stood up after me, insisting it was no problem and

they could tell I was struggling with it, and they were happy to help. I thought they were going to walk away, but then the one man, rather bluntly, asked, "Do you always go without panties?"

"Excuse me?" I responded both shocked and embarrassed.

He repeated himself, "I asked if you always go without panties? Are you teasing guys on purpose?"

Embarrassed and not knowing what to say, the other guy chimed in before I could respond.

"We were at your presentation earlier this afternoon—it was quite a show."

I began getting more embarrassed and stuttered as I tried to respond before they cut me off, "Oh, I see, I … I didn't realize I—"

"So, are you like … a stripper? Or working, if you know what I mean?"

The other guy spoke up, adding, "Cuz if you are, that's cool. Maybe you'd like to come up to our room later after you wrap up here. We're both good guys—and we'll pay."

Oh my God, they think I'm a prostitute … They think I'm here working—I guess in a way I'm not far from it with everything I've done ...

I decided not to destroy their fantasy and played along a little as I let them down.

"I'm really flattered, guys, but I fly out in a little bit so I'm just wrapping up here and I have to get to the airport soon. I appreciate the offer though."

Amusing myself that I just led these guys on to believe I was a call girl, I felt my confidence coming back until they called my bluff.

"Aawww, that sucks. Well, how about right now? There's a little storeroom over at the corner—how about just a quick blowjob. I'll give you a hundred bucks."

Oh my—what am I going to do? What do I tell them?

"I'm sorry, I can't."

"$200 then."

Are they serious? Are they offering me $200 a piece to go down on them?

Trying to talk my way out of it, I stammered back, "I'm ... sorry, that's ... a very generous offer, but I really ... I just can't right now."

"Aaww, I thought for sure that's why you were flashing us, trying to get us over here to talk to you.

Feeling like I needed to apologize, I said, "I'm sorry guys—I didn't mean to lead you on, I was just … Just having a little fun before heading out."

The one guy got a big smile on his face and then looked me right in the eye, and said, "I told Aaron you weren't gonna go for it—but he said we should try."

Feeling a weird sense of relief flood over me, I exclaimed, "Are you kidding me? He put you up to this? I'm gonna kill him," then began laughing.

The guys were chuckling along as well but then turned a little more serious as the one said, "Yeah, he put us up to it to see what you'd do, but he also said that after we told you he put us up to it, that you would do it. We just had to tell you that's what he wants you to do, and then you would."

I just stood there, shaking my head in disbelief, not even sure how to respond.

I looked at them, and then picked up my phone and said, "Give me one second."

I texted Aaron.

> Did you send two guys to see me and proposition me?

He responded quickly.

```
yes ;-) did you take them
up on their offer?
```

```
                    Nooo :-0
```

```
I wondered if you would
or not... but now that you
know, I'll be there in
about 45 min to pick you
up... they shouldn't take
that long... have fun!
```

I stood there briefly, just re-reading that a second time, mixed emotions flooding through me as I realized what he was telling me to do—what he was making me into. I remembered saying to him that I wanted to feel alive, experiment, and feel sexual—and he has given me all of that, and so much of it was outside of my comfort zone. But this, this was the furthest outside of my comfort zone I could have imagined!

Could I actually do this? I guess it's not much different than what I did with Jack the night before, I thought in some ridiculous way to try and somehow rationalize whoring myself out.

I jumped a little when I heard the one man say, "Well? You ready?"

To them, there wasn't an option—I was going to do it— Aaron told them I would do it. The man to my right put his fingers around my arm and started to lead me to walk with them. Hesitantly stepping forward, I took a deep breath, looked at them and said, "My ride's going to be here in forty minutes—this can't take long."

This is most definitely an experience I'm never going to forget—and I can't believe what I'm about to do.

They both got huge grins on their faces as they turned, and I walked with them to the back corner of the convention hall. Their names were Mike and John. Mike was a little older, handsome, but a little heavy set. John was younger, maybe even in his late twenties, fit, and looked like a farm boy. Both were wearing jeans and polo shirts.

I felt nervous and embarrassed, like someone was going to know where we were going or what we were going to do as we disappeared into the short hallway off the main room.

Stopping at the door, Mike told John to go in with me first, and he'd make sure nobody would come in. John opened the door for me, and I walked into a room about 20 ft x 20 ft with shelves and boxes scattered around. Clearly a staging area for some of the vendors at the show.

I took a few steps forward and then turned around to face John. He was wasting no time as I watched him quickly unbuckling his pants and pushing them down to his thighs, his young, hard penis sticking poker straight in front of him. He just stood there, hands on his hips, looking almost as nervous as I felt. I walked up to him, and without a word, stooped down in front of him.

Sitting my butt all the way down onto the back of my high heels, I reached up and took hold of his penis and began to stroke it, looking up to see his eyes drop shut and hear a gasp escape his mouth.

After stroking him for a few seconds with one hand, I pulled and caressed his balls with the other, then moved my hand to the base, looked up again and thought, *here goes*, and slid my lips over the head.

Another moan left his lips as I pumped him with my right hand and bobbed in and out with my mouth. I was lost in what I was doing to him as I heard him ask, "Can I see your tits?"

Without taking my lips off him, I brought my hands up to my shoulders and peeled the top of my dress down over my arms, letting my breasts come into view. I heard, "Oh fuck," quietly from his lips as I returned my hands to stroking and caressing him.

He put his left hand softly on the back of my head and reached down with his right to take one of my breasts in his palm and caress it. Despite the embarrassment of the circumstances, I was enjoying this little role play and getting aroused as I pleasured him. Without warning, he let out a moan, squeezed my breast firmly, and pulled in on my head as I felt jets of warm fluid shooting into the back of my throat.

Something about that moment—it felt so erotic doing this to a man I didn't even know, taking him in my mouth and making him cum, swallowing him. With my eyes closed, I held him deep in my mouth, moving my tongue around him until he began to soften. I slowly pulled back, letting him slip from my lips, then brought my fingers up to wipe his wetness from my chin. He took a few small steps backwards, pulling his pants up and buttoning them as I stood up and pulled the top of my dress back over my breasts. Reaching into his pocket, he pulled out two $100 bills and handed them to me.

Part of me didn't want to take it, knowing that once I did, I was now a whore. Not that my behavior the previous days was anything less, at least it was not for money.

He quietly thanked me and then turned and walked out the door. A second later, Mike came in.

Mike was a little older, a little more confident, a little more direct, and as I would soon find out, a little less of a gentleman. As he started unbuckling his pants, he asked me, "So how do you know Aaron? He your boyfriend? I see you got a ring on—he your husband?"

Softly I answered him, "No, he's not my husband, and he's not my boyfriend—I met him here."

Looking at me a little confused, he asked, "You just met him … and you're doin' shit like this for him?"

Hearing him asking me out loud made it suddenly sound as ridiculous and unbelievable as it was. Embarrassed, I answered, "Yes—but we bonded really quickly," I added in a lame effort to give some validity to the relationship I had with him.

At this point, Mike had his pants unzipped and his penis

out, slowly stroking it in front of me as he continued to question, "So when you leave today, you're never gonna see us again, or Aaron, right? You're goin' back to your husband, and your life, and pretendin' none of this ever happened, right?"

"I suppose so," I answered in a defeated, submissive tone.

A little smirk formed on his lips as he stood there staring at me, boldly stroking himself, with a smug look in his eyes.

"Take your dress off."

A little surprised, I asked, "Why? I thought I was just … going down on you."

"You are—I just don't want to get anything on your pretty dress."

Not completely believing him, I brought my fingers across to pull the string on my hip, letting it fall open, then untying the second one. Trembling slightly, I brought my fingers up and peeled the purple wrap dress back off my shoulders and let it slip down my arms, exposing my naked body to him, standing in only my black thigh-highs and high heels.

"Oh my … You are fine! Turn around—let me see you."

Feeling a little humiliated now, I slowly began to spin in

front of him as he stood there, looking me up and down with a blank stare. He continued to stroke himself, then stepped up beside me. He took hold of my wrist and moved my hand to his penis. I closed my fingers around it and began to slowly stroke him as he started running his hands over my body.

Standing to my side, his right hand was moving over my breasts as his left hand ran down my back and squeezed the naked cheeks of my ass. His right hand moved back and forth between each of my breasts, then slid down over my stomach where he pushed his fingers down between my thighs and curled one up into me. I stared straight ahead, letting deep exhales escape my lips, giving subtle jerks with my hand on his shaft as he flexed his finger, pulsing it in and out of me.

Squeezing my ass and grinding his palm and finger into me from the front, I began to respond to the stimulation as my body gave subtle little jerks to his penetration.

He leaned a little closer to my ear and said, "So you're not a whore at all—you're just some business lady—some wife— probably a mother, out of town and havin' a little fun—livin' out a fantasy, are ya?"

I didn't answer—I assumed his question was rhetorical and he already knew.

He then added, "I don't know if you realize how fuckin' hot that makes you. Way hotter than if you were a whore. Because you're not really doin' it for the money—you're doin' this because it excites you—because you like it."

I couldn't argue with what he said—he was right.

He leaned over slightly to adjust the angle of his wrist and began pumping his finger into me rapidly, causing my knees to buckle and my body to bend forward as I let out a moan.

In a condescending tone, he spoke into my ear, "Yeeeeaaahhh … There it is … You like it."

He slowed the thrusting with his hand just long enough to work a second finger into me, then pushed his left hand to the middle of my ass, pressing his fingers in against my behind also.

"Uuggghhhh," escaped my lips as he began thrusting with the fingers of his right hand again.

I was stumbling around in my high heels, trying to keep my balance as he was manhandling my body, making me cry out. I was gripping his right forearm, trying to slow and limit his movement, but he was too strong, and he just continued to pump his fingers into me. Despite all the thoughts and emotions swirling in my head, my body was responding, the sound of my wetness coating his fingers now audible. He suddenly stopped, let me catch my balance, then slid his fingers out of my pussy and brought them up to my lips. I stood there motionless for just a few seconds before I let my jaw relax and opened them slightly. He slid his fingers into my mouth—all the way—as I slowly closed my lips around his knuckles, and he stroked them in and out.

Pushing his fingers deeper into my mouth once more, he held them there as I felt him applying pressure with the finger still resting between the cheeks of my ass. Giving a moan around his fingers and wiggle of my hips to express my protest, he jerked my body against him to affirm his dominance in the situation before resuming the pressure until he penetrated me. With a longer moan that grew louder as he slipped his fingers from my lips, I stood there obediently as he dropped his hand once more between my thighs to resume fingering my pussy as well. Again, I staggered side to side as he worked both of his arms, flexing his wrists to thrust his fingers in and out of me, now in front and behind. This went on for a minute or so before he pulled his hands away and patronized, "That'a girl … Now you can suck me."

Not making eye contact, I turned and squatted down in

197

front of him. His cock was already slippery with his precum from stroking him with my hand as I leaned forward and wrapped my lips around the head.

"Yeah ... That's it, suck it baby ... Suck it good."

Unlike John, Mike was very vocal the entire time, talking to me, telling me what to do.

"Spread your legs ... Nice and wide ... Rub that pussy while you suck."

Embarrassed to admit it, I was getting more and more aroused at the way Mike was treating me and speaking to me. This wasn't me, but I was getting lost in this roleplay I'd committed myself to, letting myself experience what it feels like to be this submissive to a man, accept my purpose was purely his pleasure. Despite the demeaning tone and treatment, the entire situation was becoming so incredibly erotic to me.

When I felt Mike's hand move down into the back of my hair and tightly grip my head, I knew he was about to become more aggressive. It started slowly, but soon he was jerking my head back and then thrusting all the way forward into my throat, pressing my nose against his stomach.

He kept saying, "That's it baby ... Take it deep ... Take it all … Mmmm … Keep rubbin' that pussy."

I did everything he told me, letting him freely move my mouth on him, letting him push all the way into my throat, holding my knees spread wide as I frantically moved my fingers over my lips and clit. Wet sucking sounds escaped the corners of my mouth as he pumped himself in and out of my lips.

Just then, the door swung open, and John stepped into the room, yelling to Mike, "What's takin' so long, man? Come on!"

I instinctively startled and closed my legs, but Mike didn't miss a stroke and continued to move my head in and out as he yelled back, "Hold on—I'm almost done—just a few more minutes."

I was a little surprised as he stood there using my mouth, how nonchalant both were as I sucked him, naked and squatting in front of him with a hand between my legs.

I heard the door shut, and then Mike pulled my head back off him, saying, "Stand up."

Before I was even all the way up, he grabbed my wrist and pulled me over to a table. I didn't object as he turned me to face it and then put a hand on my back, bending me forward.

"John's gettin' impatient out there—we gotta finish up."

I was bent forward, my forearms flat on the table when I felt Mike tap the inside of my high heels with his boot, telling me to spread them a little wider. He stepped behind me, guided his penis into my pussy, and began fucking me—hard.

He wrapped one of his arms around my waist as his other hand moved up to alternate between each of my breasts, swaying freely as he thrust into me. He was grunting and breathing heavily as he slammed into me with all his weight. I too was moaning, feeling the undeniable pleasure I was longing for. He was intense and purely using my body for his pleasure, and at that moment, I loved how that felt.

He brought the hand that was around my hip up behind me and grabbed a handful of my hair, jerking my head and arching my back. Leaning forward as he ground himself deep into me, he growled in my ear, "When I tell you I'm gonna cum, I want you on your knees—got it?"

Through my heavy breathing and a moan, I answered, "Yes," but it wasn't loud enough apparently.

He thrust into me a few more times hard, then gave another jerk on the back of my hair, asking again,

200

"Understand!?"

"Yes, I understand," I said louder, almost yelling at him.

He let go of my hair and moved his hand with the other to grab my free breast. He was squeezing them tightly, using them to move my body as he increased his intensity. After about thirty seconds of this, he started to groan and then yelled at me, "Now — get on your knees!"

I pushed back enough from the table to spin my body and dropped down in front of him. As soon as my knees hit the floor, his hand was in my hair pulling me forward and sliding deep into my mouth. Just as John did, he pushed all the way to the back of my throat and held me there as he came. Still panting from the fucking I just received, I had to wait for him to finish before he released my hair, and I could take a breath.

Regaining his composure, he looked down at me with a big smile on his face, saying, "You may not be a professional, but you could have fooled me."

Just like John before him, he pulled $200 from his pocket and laid it on the table beside me.

His final comment, "Worth every penny," as he walked away.

I stood back up and made my way over to the shelf where

I laid my dress. Taking a deep breath, I tried to process what I just did. While I slipped my dress back on and wrapped it around my body, I thought to myself, *That must be what happens to call girls all the time ... They think they're doing one thing with a guy, but he makes them do more or gets rough ... I guess who are they going to tell? There's nothing they can do about it ... That's how I felt. It was a thrill to experience for me, but I can imagine how scary or uncomfortable that would be every time ...*

When I finally walked out of the room, Mike and John were gone and I made my way back toward my booth and could see Aaron standing there waiting for me. Not sure why it really mattered, but I decided not to tell Aaron what Mike just did with me. I'm just going to let him think I gave them both oral sex and was done with it.

We were looking at each other the entire time as I walked from the end of the aisle to my booth. He was just watching me, watching my body move. I felt sexual and aroused. I could feel the wetness and sensitivity from just being penetrated. I could still taste them. I could still feel Mike's fingers on my breasts. The entire day has been one moment after another exposing my body, being touched, pleasuring men and having sex, but all without a climax for me.

When I got to the booth, Aaron gave me a hug and whispered in my ear, "So, what did you think of that experience?"

I was honest with him, at least about my feelings, saying, "Honestly? It was embarrassing and humiliating, but incredibly exciting, and intense. Something I'll never forget, for sure."

He just stood there nodding as he listened, and then said, "I felt like that was something that you would find exciting, but you would have never done it on your own.

"I'll admit, it was a little scary, but it was exciting."

Aaron didn't ask for any more detail, he just turned and grabbed my bags and said, "Time to go—let's get you to the airport."

CHAPTER SIXTEEN

Heading Home

Aaron had a car waiting for us out front. It wasn't a limo this time, just a black SUV. The driver put my bags in the back and Aaron helped me into the back seat.

As we got underway, Aaron took my hand and held it in his lap as he began telling me how much he enjoyed the time we spent together, saying how special I was and that he never would have imagined meeting a woman like me. I confessed back to him that while I was fully expecting to have a little fun on this trip, I would never have imagined myself doing the things that I did.

"I feel weird in a way saying it, but I feel like I want to thank you for giving me all those experiences. It was surreal, and a time I'll never forget."

Aaron leaned over, slipped his hand up under the back of my hair and kissed me for a few seconds, passionately. I couldn't deny feeling a tingle through my body as I let my eyes fall shut and felt his soft lips pressed against mine.

He broke the kiss, leaning back a few inches and I opened my eyes as he said softly, "One last experience."

I watched his fingers move to the front of his pants as he unzipped them, reached inside and pulled out his semi hard erection. My first thought was, *the driver is right here, this isn't a limo.*

I looked forward and sure enough, the driver's eyes were darting back and forth from the road to the mirror watching us.

Aaron smiled and said, "It's okay, he knows what you're going to do."

I could feel the nervous excitement going through me once more as I gave Aaron a smile, looked in the mirror at the driver one more time, then leaned over in my seat to take him between my lips. I passionately moved my lips over him, holding his shaft with my right hand, I stroked him into my mouth. After only a few seconds, I heard Aaron's voice say, "Get up on your knees on the seat and spread your legs."

I only took my lips off him for a second as I turned my body, putting my left knee on the seat and extending my right leg down to the floor, leaning over and taking him back in my mouth.

Aaron shifted slightly to slide his right arm under the length of my body, working his hand up under the bottom of my dress to find my smooth, wet pussy and began rubbing me with his fingers. With all the stimulation I received throughout the day, I was already so wet, and so sensitive, that immediately I began responding to his touch, letting out little moans around the shaft of his cock as I bobbed up and down.

My hand and lips on Aaron, his fingers rubbing and thrusting into me, we were both building closer to our mutual orgasms. Both of us were moaning and letting out sighs as I suddenly felt something touching my leg that was extended down behind the seat. I turned my head slightly, still sliding my lips up and down his shaft. I looked over to the right and saw the driver's arm extended down behind the seat.

Apparently, this intense situation playing out right behind him was too much for him to ignore or be content to just watch.

He was making a connection, sliding his hand up and down my calf, feeling the sheer black nylon of my thigh-highs. It was only a hand on my calf, but somehow it intensified the situation for me even further, being touched by two men at the same time.

Knowing the ride would be over soon, I focused my attention back on pleasuring Aaron, getting him to his orgasm. My final act for him. The motion of his hand between my legs, and the way he was moving his hips up towards my mouth told me he was ready to explode. I heard him begin to let out a low groan and felt his free hand move to the back of my head. He was cumming.

Feeling him pulsing in my mouth, the taste of his hot release over my tongue, his fingers between my legs, a hand now caressing my entire leg and up the back of my thigh, and a day of teasing—it was all more than enough to put me over the edge as an orgasm rippled through my body at the same time. I struggled to swallow and take all of him as I cried out with my own warm sensations rippling through my body. I could vaguely feel the driver's hand move all the way up the back of my leg—under my dress—to squeeze and explore the bare right cheek of my ass as I came.

I held this position for another moment, just relaxing, gently sucking and savoring Aaron in my mouth, feeling his fingers between my legs now also gently slipping in and out of me in a massaging way, and the driver's hand now moved back down to softly caress my calf.

Slowly lifting my head, I gave a final kiss and swirl of my tongue around the tip of Aaron's cock before pushing myself back up and turning in my seat. As I did, I watched the driver pull his arm back up between the seats, still intently looking at me in the mirror as I briefly made eye contact with him, then turned my attention back to Aaron.

Aaron stared at me with a content look on his face, smiling and saying, "That was one hell of a goodbye kiss. I'm not going to forget our time together anytime soon. Thank you for indulging my fantasies. I hope you were able to experience some of your own as well."

"Yes, it has been quite an incredible few days. I've honestly not given myself time to process everything that's happened these past few days, and so much of it was more than I ever would have imagined I would do, but I don't regret any of it, it was so ... hot," I replied, just shaking my head and giving a little laugh.

We pulled up to the curb at the drop off area for the terminal. Our driver jumped out and hurried around to open my door, intently watching me as I turned my legs in his direction and slid out of my seat. He offered a hand to steady me as I slid down out of the SUV, the entire time, intently enjoying my dress sliding up and parting briefly to reveal my thigh-highs and bare skin above.

I gave him a small, embarrassed smile, thinking about what he just watched me do and how he caressed my leg as I experienced my orgasm. It was such an intimate experience to have right in front of a stranger, and then to stand face to face with them right after was embarrassing and erotic. He just gave me a little smile back and nodded, then hurried to the back to get my bags.

Aaron came around and put his hands on my hips, staring intently into my eyes, telling me, "Thank you for everything, you're an amazing woman. I know you have to go back to your life, and put all this behind you, but perhaps our paths will cross again someday."

Just as I said, "Perhaps," he leaned down and passionately kissed me, thrusting his tongue between my lips as his hands slid to the top of my ass and squeezed my body tight against him.

After a few seconds of this embrace, he released me and stepped back, saying, "Goodbye."

Licking my lips and catching my breath, I simply said, "Bye," then turned to walk into the terminal.

I made my way through checking my bags and the security checkpoint with no holdups. I remember joking to myself as I stood in the full body scanner at security, *there's definitely nothing to see under my dress.*

Now sitting at my gate, I finally felt myself coming down from the sexual high I'd been riding for so many days. Seeing my home airport up on the boarding sign was bringing reality back that it was time to return to normal life.

I experienced one more moment of exposure, on the plane. It wasn't a long flight, only a couple of hours, but about thirty minutes in I fell asleep. I must have squirmed a little in my seat, trying to get comfortable, and in the process the bottom of my dress completely opened, revealing my lack of panties. As I woke up, before I noticed my revealed state, I looked around and the man sitting beside me was staring down at my legs. His wife was beside him, but she was also asleep, allowing him to enjoy his fortunate surroundings.

When I looked down to see what he was staring at, my entire left leg was completely exposed all the way to the top of my thigh, almost to my hip. The only thing possibly hiding my pussy from his view was the top wrap of my dress stretched over from the tie at my hip, barely covering me, however I was pretty sure if he leaned forward a few inches in his seat he would be able to see me. I also noticed both of his hands were down resting on his knees in the tight seat, but the last two fingers of his right hand were on the side of his leg and pressed against the outside of my thigh, feeling the texture of my sheer thigh-highs.

He hadn't even noticed that I woke up or saw any of this, so I didn't want to make an embarrassing situation more obvious, or make him feel caught, so I continued to sit there, pretending to be asleep for quite a while longer. And I won't deny that as I sat there pretending to sleep, I may have pressed my left thigh against his fingers a few times, and I felt him move them slightly against me.

I had no way of knowing, but my intuition was telling me

he was a "leg man", the way he was mesmerized by my revealing position, and I think that even that subtle connection to my sheer hosiery on my leg was driving him crazy.

When the pilot came over the speaker making an announcement, I pretended to wake up and then casually sat up and pulled my dress back over my legs as I crossed them, not acknowledging that he saw anything. I laughed to myself when I began to move and he quickly pulled his right hand away from my leg, up to the side of his face to pretend to scratch his cheek. I then turned to him and in a friendly tone asked, "Are we landing soon?" pretending to be unaware of anything that just transpired and set him at ease.

I could tell he was nervous when he looked at me and said, "Uhh, I think—like twenty minutes." I just smiled and turned to look out the window for the remainder of the flight.

By the time my flight landed, I retrieved my bags, and made it home, it would be after midnight. My husband was already in bed but still awake waiting for me since I texted him when I left the airport to let him know everything was fine. While I drove home, I was already starting to feel the weight of guilty thoughts beginning to set in. I knew what I did was so bad, and disrespectful in so many ways to my husband, but I became swept up in the excitement of experiencing so many erotic emotions and situations that I couldn't stop.

I didn't know how my husband was going to greet me when I got there and started to worry that he might discover I'm wearing thigh-highs and no underwear and question it, so I came up with a lie just in case. Before I got home, I slipped off my black thigh-highs and put them in my purse, leaving me now with only my high heels and purple wrap dress. I made my way upstairs and into the bedroom, lugging my bags along behind me. I walked over to the edge of the bed and leaned down to give him a kiss and he asked how my trip was. I stood there, briefly telling him it was good, and I made a lot of contacts as I felt him drop his hand down to the back of my thigh and start sliding it up and down, telling me he missed me.

I said I missed him too as I felt him slide his hand all the way up to give my bare bottom a squeeze. He paused for a second then started moving his fingers around and looked at me asking, "Are you not wearing underwear?"

With my response already crafted, I lied, "No, when I got

to the airport my luggage got caught on my pantyhose and ripped the entire leg open, so I had to take them off and didn't have time to dig out a new pair, so I just went without."

He got a big smile on his face and replied, "So … the entire flight and walking through the airport you didn't have underwear on? That's really hot!"

Ohhh, you have no idea …

"Glad you think so! It was exciting, and it made me a little nervous because I felt naked the entire time. Now let me go get a shower—I feel gross from traveling all day."

Standing in the shower, feeling the hot water running over my face and down my body, I continued struggling with the emotions of my week.

I hate lying to him—I feel like I need to go in there and do anything he wants …

I dried myself off and slipped on a short silk nightie, then climbed into bed with my husband, curling up next to him. He turned towards me and kissed me, running his hands over my body and loving me. Only making my guilt heavier, I whispered to him, "Let me do something for you—what do you want? Whatever you want—anything."

"Wow, anything? I need to think about this for a second,"

he responded, joking with me, "but if you're tired, we can just go to sleep."

Way to be sweet and just make me feel even worse …

"How about I just go down on you now, and then whenever you want to cash in my 'anything' offer, just let me know."

"Mmmm, I'm not going to argue with that."

After giving him another kiss, I pushed the covers down and worked him free from his boxers. Within a few minutes I had him full of life and standing at attention, pumping my hand on his shaft and bobbing my head over the tip. It didn't take long before he was ready to explode, and as usual, he gave me plenty of warning, pulling his shirt up to give me a place to let him spray. Typically, that's where I would direct him, but not tonight, not with how I felt.

"I'm gonna cum … I'm gonna cum!" breathily escaped his lips as he brought his hand down to direct his penis up towards his stomach, but I lifted my head up, looked into his eyes and said, "No—I want to taste you—let me swallow you."

I know that's something he often desires, but not usually what happens, so as soon as I said that it put him over the edge. I wrapped my lips around him just in time to feel him begin to release. His entire body tensed while I kept my lips sealed around him, pumping him into my mouth.

A long groan escaped his throat as his body writhed on the bed until he finished. I continued to savor and caress him, my eyes closed, and my mouth gently moving over the soft skin of his head, getting every last drop of him. I slipped him from my lips and tucked him back into his boxers, then moved up to lay my head on his chest, saying, "I'm sorry I was gone so long."

Over the next couple days, life returned to routine, and I put my trip behind me and on a shelf. However, I was reminded of everything Monday morning when I went into work. Not long after getting into my day, a package was brought up to my desk—it was my underwear. I made sure no one was around and opened the box to peek in. Sure enough, there were all my bras, panties, and pantyhose stuffed into this box, but laying right on top was a business card.

It was Aaron's card with all his contact info, and on the back was written, "Thank you for our time ... hope to see you next year!"

I don't believe our company had a booth again at that conference—and it wasn't my role anyway, I was just the last-minute substitution. Did I consider connecting with Aaron again? I'd be lying if I said I didn't. There were many times that I let my mind drift back to the things that happened to me during the show, fueling fantasies and intense orgasms during masturbation. I know it all happened; I lived it. But it was such an unreal, fantasy-like sequence of events, I still find it hard to believe that I let myself get caught up that way and actually did all of those things. And it was all because of Aaron.

He orchestrated so much of it, making me his muse, using my desire to experiment erotically. He put me in situation after situation that pushed my limits of comfort but resulted in the most intensely arousing experiences I'd ever had. How do I make peace with myself—for my marriage, and my husband—knowing the things I've done? Right or wrong, for better or worse, I tell myself that as erotic as everything I experienced felt, none of it was from a place of love—it was purely physical. I love my husband.

I'm not looking to put myself in that position again or trying to find a way to recreate it, but I won't deny that given the opportunity, with the right circumstances, I wouldn't give in to those desires once more. That's why I never reached out to Aaron again. I don't love Aaron. I don't need Aaron in my life, but the things that Aaron could make me do, I can't trust the decisions I'd make—or be able to deny that hidden side of myself.

CONFESSION THREE:

My Meeting with Robert, College Memories, and a Gift to My Husband

CHAPTER SEVENTEEN

A Surprising Referral

I can count on one hand the number of times I've been truly surprised by a situation when I've gone to meet with a client, this story is one of them.

Although we make cold calls and get new clients from our marketing and advertising, referrals make up a huge percentage of our new clients. I received an email from the executive assistant to the CEO for one of the East Coast's larger resort and hotel companies. They owned resort properties and hotels in most of the major tourist destinations and larger cities.

She wanted me to call about setting up an appointment with Mr. Robert Duncan. That was the first surprise. Typically, the CEO of a multibillion-dollar company isn't the one you meet with to talk about stationery and toilet paper supplies. Nonetheless, I'm not going to look a gift horse in the mouth, so I called and set everything up. Mr. Duncan was going to be at one of their properties in a city on the other side of the state, so I had to go for an overnight trip.

This had the potential to be a huge contract for my company, and the commissions I could see from it would be more than I'd ever earned. Of course, we would be providing all the office supplies and equipment for the front desks and back offices, but our company also provides cleaning products and other paper products, which in the hotel industry is huge.

Mr. Duncan's assistant informed me that he would be meeting with me in the evening on the day that I arrived, and I would be joining him for dinner at the property's five-star restaurant. They also provided me with a complimentary room for the night.

Ninety-five percent of the time this job is buried in paperwork and trudging from little back office to back office—nothing glamorous or exciting. This was one of those rare cases where I got to go and wine and dine with the client. Knowing it was a five-hour drive, I left around nine A.M. so I didn't have to rush. I was in my room by three and able to relax and take my time getting ready for dinner.

The room was definitely an upgrade from a normal hotel room. It was on one of the higher floors with a nice view of the city, a large king bed and a full living room area, but I was most impressed with the bathroom and the large jacuzzi tub. I thought it was amusing that I was the one trying to get him as a client, but he was pampering me.

I ran a wonderfully hot bubble bath, dimmed the lights, slipped out of my dress, pantyhose and bra, and slid into the tub to relax. Whenever I have to travel for work, I always try to make the most of it and take a little time for myself, even if it is just an overnight escape. As I lay back in the water, feeling the bubbles dancing around my breasts and cleavage, I pulled my feet in and relaxed my hips open, letting my fingers glide over my inner thighs.

There's something about driving for hours on the highway—I don't know what it is—but it makes me ... horny. Maybe it's just the time to relax and let my mind wander with the hum of the road in the background and the wind, or maybe it's knowing I'm traveling to a new place where no one knows me, and I can let go a little. It was only a short time after a few deep relaxing breaths that my eyes were shut, feeling the warmth of the water around me, and my fingers slipped between my legs to gently caress.

The middle and ring fingers of my right hand were effortlessly gliding between my lips, sliding all the way down between the cheeks of my ass, and then back up to make a small circle over my clit and repeat the motion. My left hand was caressing my breasts, squeezing and massaging, my fingers circling my nipples and then pinching and pulling at them to tease myself.

Mmmhhhh … This feels so nice …

After only a few minutes, I brought myself to an orgasm. I could hear my moans echoing off the hard tile and marble in the bathroom as my back arched and I squeezed my thighs together, trapping my hand between my legs with my finger pressing down on my clit. The thumb and forefinger of my left hand clamped down hard on my right nipple, squeezing and twisting it as the delightful feelings swept through my body.

Almost falling asleep as I relaxed a few minutes longer, I finally pushed myself up out of the tub, dried off, and then wrapped my body in the towel. After touching up my hair and makeup, I walked out to pick up my bag and lay out my clothes.

Before I started dressing, I had the strangest desire to walk over and stand in the window, just staring out at the city beneath me. As I looked down and saw cars zipping through the streets and the little people scampering around, I brought my fingers up to loosen the top of the towel and let it fall from my body. I felt nervous excitement standing there in the window, in full view of anyone who might be looking, imagining strangers down below, or in other buildings watching as I parade in front of them.

I brought both of my arms up, stretching and then running my fingers through the back of my hair, pushing my breasts out and imagining their eyes moving over me. It felt sexy, and naughty, putting myself on display this way. With a slow turn, I walked back toward the bed, seductively swaying my hips and imagined their disappointment as I moved out of view and began to get dressed.

Knowing the potential for this account and sitting down with a multi-millionaire in one of his hotel's five-star restaurants, I certainly wanted to leave nothing to chance with my wardrobe selection. I selected an elegant black spaghetti strap, silky wrap dress that fell just above my knees. A single bow on my left hip held the dress loosely wrapped around my body, creating a plunging V between my breasts, and letting the bottom of the dress part open slightly as I walked and sat.

Underneath was a black garter belt attached to barely there, sheer nude thigh-high stockings, and a very delicate black sheer and lace g-string panty pulled over top. Completing the outfit were my black slingback Louboutin high heels. My choice of underwear was just as much for me as it potentially was for him. I wasn't assuming anything was going to happen, but I surely wanted to make an impression if it did. Also, for me at least, when I feel sexy, I feel confident, and wearing a garter belt and stockings with barely-there panties under such a silky material definitely feels sexy.

I picked up my clutch and my phone and made a last spin in front of the mirror. Immediately, I was aware of the silky material moving over my naked breasts and nipples as I turned, adding just another layer of sensation, arousing them and adding to their impression through the material.

Yeah, this outfit should get his attention ...

CHAPTER EIGHTEEN

Dinner With Robert,

and ...

I made my way up to the restaurant; it was on one of the uppermost floors of the hotel. The hostess was expecting me and led me to a table on an elevated level at the back of the restaurant, right against floor-to-ceiling windows that gave an amazing view over the city. As I carefully made my way up the steps, I saw Mr. Duncan standing at his table to greet me. I was a little surprised to see that his wife had joined us.

I'd seen pictures of him online but meeting him in person, he was much taller than I expected, well over six feet. He was in his late forties, distinguished but almost intimidating looking with his strong features and bald head. His suit—no doubt costing as much as my car—was black and clearly custom tailored, with a white button-up shirt and gold tie.

As I approached him, he stepped forward to greet me, shaking my hand, but then also pulling me in to give a kiss on my cheek and embrace me. His wife stood also and stepped around the table to greet me in the same way.

She was beautiful. Barely in her twenties, she looked as if she could have stepped out of a glamor magazine with her long flowing blonde hair, full lips, thin features, and high cheekbones. I was feeling sexy and confident, and knew I looked good, but standing next to her I began to feel a little intimidated.

She was wearing a deep blue, cowl neck, drape style dress that wrapped around her body and barely made it to the middle of her thigh. The front of her dress fell deep across her breasts, barely covering her nipples but exposed a surprising amount of cleavage and the inner curve of her breasts. The back was open all the way down to the bottom of her tailbone, nearly exposing the crack of her behind, but showing more than enough to know she wasn't wearing panties. Her legs were bare, tanned and silky, and on her feet, she wore four-inch high-heeled sandals in a camel color.

So, this is what they call a trophy wife ...

We sat and talked for a while, enjoying some cocktails, but anytime that I tried to discuss work, he said there would be time to talk about that later, and seemed more interested in me and my life. His wife was pleasant and engaging, but I quickly picked up on the flirtatious looks and leg crossing she was directing toward a cute guy sitting at the end of the bar.

I was surprised at how obvious some of the flirting was, but Robert didn't seem to pay any attention to it—he was clearly focused on me. As we sat and talked, waiting for our meals to arrive, Robert extended his hand over and placed it on my knee under the table, lightly stroking his fingers over it and up to the hem of my dress. I made no effort to draw attention to it and acted as if it was perfectly normal.

Our dinners arrived, and I must admit, it was probably one of the best meals I've ever had. Everything was done to perfection, and the petite filet that I ordered melted in my mouth. After dinner, the table was cleared, and we enjoyed another round of martinis. Robert's hand returned to my leg, only this time slightly higher, pushing the hem of my dress enough to let his fingers rest on the lace at the top of my stockings. When he felt that, he gave a little smile, continuing to run his fingers back and forth over it.

It was at about this time that he turned to his wife and said, "Honey, we need to discuss some business, no need for you to sit here and be bored, why don't you go and enjoy yourself."

She finished her martini and then stood up to walk around the table. Leaning down, she gave him a kiss on the cheek and told him she loved him, then turned to me, taking my hand in hers, she said, "And it was very nice to meet you, I look forward to seeing you again," and off she walked.

Robert could clearly see the confusion on my face as I watched her walk across the room and climb up onto the stool next to the man she'd been flirting with all evening. When I looked back at him, he was just smiling and said, "We have a very open relationship. We love each other, but I let her have her fun, and she lets me have mine."

His hand gave a very intent move up and down my thigh as he said that, indicating that I was that fun. With a little smirk, he followed up with, "I do know we have to talk about some business tonight, so let's get that out of the way, shall we?"

His hand never left my thigh for the next thirty minutes, but we did cover all the major points of the proposed contract. As we were finishing up, I asked, "You never told me who referred you—was it another one of my clients?"

He went on to tell me that one of his dearest and oldest friends that he went through college with was one of my clients, and he strongly recommended me if he was ever in need of my company's services. As soon as he told me who his friend was, I immediately knew why he called me. It's definitely a story for another time, but my relationship with his old college friend involved providing a very high level of personalized service ... in his office ... with my lips.

Don't get me wrong, this was a legitimate business deal, and he was intent on signing a contract with us, but now there was no doubt about what else he was anticipating that night.

After he finished telling me about his friend, he finished his drink and then stood up, took my hand, and said, "Why don't we go up to my suite, we can continue our discussion there in a more private setting."

At this point, to take that in any other way than, "come up to my room so I can fuck you," would have been very naive.

As we walked out, I noticed he nodded to his wife at the bar, and she just smiled and returned the nod. I asked if she was staying there and he replied, "I have a feeling she's going to be occupied for the next couple hours."

CHAPTER NINETEEN

The Sweetest Suite

It was a short walk to the elevator, and then only up a couple floors to his penthouse suite. I've been in hotel suites before, and penthouses, but this one was impressive. Ornate woodworking, beautiful marble, and elegant accent lighting— every detail looked to be done with the finest craftsmanship, and the entire outside wall had the same floor to ceiling windows with the incredible view of the city.

There was light jazz playing in the background as I wandered around looking at the artwork, and Robert made us a couple more drinks at the bar. Proposing a toast, he handed me another martini and we clinked our glasses to the beginning of a mutually beneficial relationship. Throughout the entire evening, he was very much the gentleman, very thoughtful and calming, but still with a strong presence.

We continued to talk business, but I know both of us could feel the sexual tension growing in the room. He knew why I came up to his room, and I knew why he wanted me to come up to his room. We were standing in the window, looking out over the city as he pointed out the sights below. I could smell his cologne as he leaned down close beside my head, his fingers lightly moving over my exposed skin on my back and shoulder as he would point in front of me with his other hand.

He took my glass and set it to the side on a table, then stepped behind me, placing his large hands on the outside of my shoulders. Continuing to talk to me about one of the older buildings out in front of us, I could feel his body begin to lightly touch mine from behind and I could see our reflection in the glass in front of me.

He stood a foot taller than me, towering over me in the reflection as I watched his hands moving slowly up and down the outside of my arms. Simultaneously, I watched and felt his fingers move all the way up over the tops of my shoulders to the thin black spaghetti straps of my dress. As if he was testing me, he took the thin straps between his thumb and finger, lifting up slightly on them and pulling them out over the top corners of my shoulders, he held them there for a few seconds. It was like he was giving me the time to stop him or say "no", but I didn't.

After his pause, he so very slowly began lowering his hands, taking the straps of my dress with them until they were draped down around my wrists and my breasts were revealed in the reflection in front of us. My breathing was shallow, and I could feel the cool air of the room moving over my nipples, anxiously awaiting his next move.

He slipped his hands around the front of my hips and that sent a chill through my body as his fingertips moved over the exposed skin of my stomach, up my ribs, until he opened his hands to cup the undersides of my breasts in each of them. My eyes fell shut and my head rested back against his chest when he dropped his lips down to my shoulder and began to kiss my bare skin. His hands began to squeeze and explore my breasts and nipples, and his mouth kissed and nibbled its way over my shoulder to my neck and up to my ear, taking my breath away.

Working my hands back between our bodies, I began stroking his growing erection through the front of his pants. Immediately, I realized he wasn't wearing underwear, so I found his zipper and then slipped my hand inside. Still kissing my neck and mauling my breasts with his right hand, he dropped his left hand down to untie my dress and let it fall from my body.

I opened my eyes, seeing the reflection of my exposed body in the glass, and then looked out to the city beyond. I remembered just a few hours before, standing in my room, naked in the window and imagining the strangers watching me from below.

I wonder if any of them are watching now?

Just as I stood there thinking that, I felt him step back slightly, his fingers tracing down my ribs, over my hips, to push my panties down my legs, letting them fall around my ankles so I could step out of them. I didn't look back, but I had a feeling that was confirmed in only a few seconds. Moving my body forward, he pressed me against the glass and then I felt him pressing between my legs.

I spread my feet and arched my back slightly, trying to improve his angle as he found the opening of my pussy with the head of his cock. He rubbed it back and forth, teasing me, penetrating me with just the tip and then pulling it back out. Finally, on the fourth or fifth penetration like this, he pushed forward and slid his entire length into me.

"Uuuuhhhh," escaped my throat as he pinned my hips to the glass and began thrusting himself into me. It felt so good — so raw and carnal — and I felt so exposed, on display in the window for the world to see as he fucked me. Suddenly, he slid out and spun me around, pushing my back against the window. Reaching down with his left hand, he hooked the back of my right knee and raised my leg up and out to the side, opening my hips as I balanced on one foot.

Holding his erection by the base of the shaft, he lowered his hips and then guided himself back up into me from the front. Once inside, he began a steady pulse of his hips as he leaned down and pressed his lips against mine, driving his tongue into my mouth and passionately kissing me. I could feel his right hand fondling my breast as we kissed, and the front of his pelvis pushing in against mine with each thrust of his hips.

Just as quickly as he started, he broke the kiss, slid out of me and lowered my leg down, stepping back to admire me in the window.

"Oh fuck … You look hot! What a sexy little body you have. Come on, let's go to the bedroom."

Grabbing my wrist with his strong hand, he quickly pulled me along behind him, through the living room, down a short hall and into the master bedroom. Once inside, he turned around and stood with his arms out looking at me with a smile and said, "Undress me."

I stepped forward, looking at him seductively as I brought my fingers up to loosen and remove his tie, then began unbuttoning the front of his shirt. Pulling it up out of his pants, I pushed it back over his shoulders, revealing a very fit and toned chest and stomach. Now moving my fingers to his belt buckle, I opened it and unbuttoned his pants. I couldn't help but give a few teasing brushes of my fingers over his penis as it stuck out from his zipper. He kicked his shoes off, and I slipped his pants down and helped him step out of them and his socks. Now naked, he slid onto the bed, laid back in the middle, spreading his legs and taking his erection in his hand to slowly stroke it.

"Come wrap your lips around me," was all he said.

I climbed onto the bed from the bottom, laying on my stomach between his spread legs and positioned myself to take him in my hands and lower my lips around him. Bending my knees and crossing my ankles, I waved my high heels up behind my naked ass as I bobbed my head up and down on him in a playful position.

"Aaahh ... that's it baby, work my cock ... Suck it deep."

He continued to moan, make subtle comments and give directions, as I laid there taking my time to pleasure him. I used my mouth on him for at least ten minutes, exploring every inch of his shaft with my lips and tongue, taking him deep at times. When I saw his hands come down and touch my forearms, I looked up and he instructed me, "Come up here and ride me."

I pushed myself up to my hands and knees and then crawled forward up over his hips. Once my hips were over top of his erection, I straightened up on my knees and then reached between my legs to guide him. He put his hands on the front of my thighs, caressing them and the sheer nylon of my stockings as I slowly pushed my knees apart, lowering myself down on to him.

Now in control, I put my hands on his muscular chest and began grinding my hips into him, riding him as we stared into each other's eyes.

He kept saying "harder" and "faster", staring intensely at me as he watched me obey his commands and drive myself to an orgasm. I cried out as my body convulsed on top of his, falling down to press my breasts against his chest and bury my face against his neck, slowly gyrating my hips to continue stimulating myself.

Being so much stronger than me, he easily pushed my body up and over to the side, slid off the bed and walked around to me. He slid me over to the edge of the bed and stood me up, my legs still trembling from my orgasm as I stumbled in my high heels. Turning me around, he had me stand a few feet from the bed, my feet spread wide and bent forward at the waist putting my forearms down on the bed. After taking a moment to caress my thighs and the cheeks of my ass, he stepped in behind me and entered me once more. I could feel the strong grip of his fingers holding my hips as he pounded into me, evoking a steady moan from my throat.

I was so lost in the intense feelings going through my body, that I was totally oblivious to my surroundings. Still pushed all the way inside of me, he reached forward to grab my biceps and stood me up in front of him. Turning me slightly, he held my body tight against his, holding me up on my tiptoes, even in my high heels. With one arm around my midsection and the other slightly above it, his hand groping my breast, the way he was holding me up and continuing to thrust into me, it was like I was being impaled on his erection. The angle he was penetrating me felt incredible! My head was laying back on his shoulder, my eyes closed and my mouth open as I cried out, letting him use my body like a rag doll. This went on for a few minutes before he slowed his pace, and I brought my head forward. That's when I opened my eyes.

Oh fuck!

CHAPTER TWENTY

Two's Company, Three's a ...

I immediately felt an anxious panic. There I was, wearing only my stockings, garter belt and high heels, my arms pulled back and my breasts pushed out, being fucked in this standing position in the middle of the room, as his wife stood in the doorway of the bedroom watching. Robert continued to fuck me this way as I just let him move my body, not knowing what to say or do. Our eyes were locked, and I was trying to read her expression, but it was blank.

Suddenly Robert stopped, noticing his wife, and put his lips beside my ear, "It seems we have an audience."

He didn't seem concerned or worried at all that she walked in on us. He began slowly grinding his hips into me again while Alison walked forward until she was standing right in front of me. It's hard to describe what I felt in that moment, naked, being penetrated by a man behind me, standing face to face with his wife, wondering what she's going to do.

My arms were still trapped under Robert's tight grip, so I was completely vulnerable as I watched her raise her hand. Somehow, I was fully convinced that she was going to slap me, so you can imagine my surprise when she brought her hand forward and began tracing her finger around my breast and over my nipple.

A small smile formed on her lips as she delicately moved her finger up between my breasts, to my neck, and then up to my cheek. I felt her fingers slip around the back of my neck into my hair, and then she leaned forward, closing her eyes, she pressed her lips against mine and began to kiss me.

I was shocked at first, surprised that this was what she was doing, but then as I felt Robert intensify his thrusts again, I let my eyes close and began to respond to her touch and kiss. It immediately flashed me back to memories of college and the last time I was ever touched or kissed by a woman.

I could feel my body growing closer to a second orgasm as I began losing myself in this intimate kiss with this beautiful young woman. Our tongues danced with each other and her fingers caressed my breast and the back of my neck with a tenderness only a woman would have. Breaking the kiss, she slowly stepped back, continuing to smile at me as I watched her bring her fingers up to the top of her dress on her shoulders. In one slow motion, she pulled the top of her dress out over her shoulders and let it slide down her body, revealing her breasts, slipping it over her hips, her thighs, and then falling to the floor around her high heels. Just as I assumed, she was naked under her dress. Her hips were thin and her stomach flat and toned. Her breasts were slightly smaller than mine, with the perkiest little brown nipples pointing straight out.

Now naked, she stepped back in to press her body against mine, returning her lips to kiss me as her husband continued to fucked me from behind. Robert released my arms and stepped away, walking around us and admiring our bodies pressed against each other as she continued to kiss me, now with her hands roaming my back and ass as she held me tight against her body.

Stepping in close, Robert ran his hands up and down both of our backs, squeezing the cheeks of our asses and caressing our bodies. Alison broke away from the kiss and turned to kiss him for a moment before Robert moved us over to the bed.

Robert had me lay in the middle of the bed on my back, then pulled me to the edge so my head hung off of the bed. I watched him take his erection in his hand and then step forward to guide it into my mouth. With my head hung back in this position, he was able to easily stroke himself all the way into the back of my throat. The first couple times he nearly gagged me, but then I was able to relax and let him freely slide all the way in and out of my mouth.

I reached up behind him with my hands to caress the tight cheeks of his ass and the back of his thighs as he used my mouth for his pleasure. That's when I felt hands on my ankles sliding them apart, opening my legs wide. With my head hung back, I couldn't see anything, and Robert was continuing with a slow but steady rhythm sliding his shaft in and out of my mouth.

I knew it was Alison as I felt her thin fingers tracing their way up my stocking covered legs. She caressed all the way up the inside of my thighs, to the exposed skin above my stockings, and then up over my hip bones before letting her fingers graze down over the smooth lips of my pussy. Her touch was gone for only a few seconds and then I felt her long blonde hair tickling the inside of my thighs, followed by her soft lips pressed against me.

I could tell immediately the difference of a woman doing this to me. Every movement and touch of her lips and tongue was deliberate but soft and gentle, almost loving. She pressed her lips against me, kissing me as if she was kissing my other set of lips. When her tongue slipped between them, I could immediately tell she knew exactly where to caress. Within a few moments, she had my hips gyrating against her mouth and wet moans of pleasure escaping around Robert's shaft as he slowly slid in and out of my lips. And as if I wasn't experiencing enough, Robert would reach down and take hold of my nipples, pinching them and pulling up on them before suddenly letting them go, sending a jolt directly between my legs every time. Together, they worked my body until they brought me to another orgasm. I can only imagine

251

what a sight that was to see me in that position, squirming beneath the two of them.

I could taste the precum oozing from the tip of Robert's penis and thought for sure he was going to let go and release in my mouth, but he didn't. Robert pushed forward one last time, as deep into my throat as he could. I could feel his hands caressing my neck, feeling the bulge of his penis as his shaved testicles rested lewdly against my face.

He held there just long enough to make me begin to squirm, needing to take a breath. Swiftly pulling all the way out of my mouth, I gasped and let out a few coughs as I picked my head up just in time to see Alison moving from between my legs.

She reached for my hand and pulled me, turning me to lay on my side in the middle of the bed. I was in such a relaxed state from my orgasm and all of the stimulation I'd received, I instinctively curled up on my side as she climbed into the bed and laid down facing me. Our bodies intertwined and she took me in her arms, our naked breasts pressed against each other, and our lips meeting in this embrace.

My eyes were closed, and I was letting myself experience this moment with another woman to the fullest. I opened my eyes slightly when I felt Alison's body begin rocking against me. Robert had climbed into the bed behind her and was now fucking her. Our lips continued to stay pressed together as I heard little moans and whimpers escaping into my mouth from hers. There was something so erotic and sensual about being this close to her and experiencing her pleasure that way. Without thinking, I slid my fingers up to begin caressing her breast, pinching and rolling her nipple the way I like to have my mine stimulated. When I felt her body laying still, I opened my eyes again to see that Robert was gone, but I realized where he was soon enough as I felt him climbing onto the bed behind me now.

Alison's eyes were open now as well, looking deeply into mine, watching my expression and emotion as her husband pushed into me and began rocking my body into hers. She watched me for a few seconds before pressing her lips back against mine to continue the kiss, this time on the receiving end of my moans and whimpers. She began driving her tongue into my mouth and I instinctively started to suck on it. Her hand was also down between us, her fingers rubbing my clit as her husband thrust into me from behind. It all felt so good!

Robert fucked me this way for only a few minutes before I felt him slide out and pull back on my hips, rolling me onto my back. He positioned himself on his knees between my legs, pushing them open wide, bent at the knees and up over his so he could enter me. He jerked my body towards him by my thighs, pushing himself all the way back into me and starting a steady rhythm.

Alison was up on her knees to my side, running her palms over my breasts and stomach, then leaning over to kiss her husband as he fucked me. I just laid there on my back, letting out little whimpers as he drove into me, watching them passionately kissing and sharing the moment. I remember thinking, *He's making love to his wife and just using my body for his pleasure.*

After a few moments of this, Robert broke the kiss and whispered something in his wife's ear. Alison smiled at him, and looked down at me, into my eyes, as I watched her turn and move up to swing her leg over my body and position herself over my face.

I'll be honest, a nervous uncertainty went through my mind as I watched her lower the smooth lips of her pussy down towards my mouth. She gently pressed herself against my lips, and after a few seconds of doubt, I opened my mouth and slipped my tongue up between the soft folds of her lips, parting them and moving it up until I found her clit. I began flicking it back and forth, then slowing and tracing small circles as I felt her begin to ever so slowly gyrate her hips.

For a short time, I was so engrossed with the feeling of my tongue pressed against this beautiful young woman that I almost forgot Robert was fucking me. I was quickly reminded when I felt Robert's hands hook under the back of my knees and roll my hips back, followed by an intense pounding forward of his hips.

I began letting out moans, but they were muffled by Alison's soft lips pressed against my mouth. Robert's thrusting was rocking my body forward and backwards slightly, adding to the motion of my tongue pressed into Alison. As I continued to lick, I could see Alison's head fall back, arching her back and pushing her firm young breasts out while a steady low moan emanated from her throat. Robert slipped a hand up around her and began fondling her breast as she steadily increased the pressure and intensity, grinding her pussy against my mouth. Feeling the erotism of the entire situation, I too was losing myself in the moment, feeling Roberts thrusts, watching the pleasure rippling through Alison's body, and feeling her urgency against my lips. I moved my tongue down and thrust it into her as deep as I could several times before returning to her clit.

The movement of her hips became erratic, and her moans turned into a cry as an orgasm shuddered through her body. I recognized the sweet taste as she came, similar to that of my own that I had experienced so many times before from my fingers or on the shaft of a lover. She continued to slowly move her hips, the occasional shudder passing through her body as she tipped her head forward and looked intensely down at me. Knowing the high sensitivity that a woman experiences after an oral orgasm, I slowed the movement of my tongue to a gentle caress. I could see she was making herself hold her position, struggling against the continued caress of my tongue, no matter how subtle. With a gasp, she finally pushed up with her knees, pulling herself from my lips and climbing off of me.

I could feel her wetness coating my lips and chin, but before I could bring my hand up to wipe it, she dropped down and passionately kissed me, savoring and showing her appreciation for my act of pleasure. While we kissed, I could feel Robert moving from between my legs and lowering them down.

When Alison broke the kiss and raised up, I could see Robert standing beside the bed, just staring at us and appreciating our intimacy. Alison pushed back off the bed and then took my hand, guiding me off and in front of Robert, then pulled me down to join her on our knees in front of him.

Robert stepped forward, his erection still hard and twitching, glistening with my juices, and putting it just a few inches in front of my face. Alison reached up and wrapped her delicate fingers around the shaft and began pumping it with a forceful stroke from the base to the head. I could hear the wetness coating her fingers as she stroked him. I glanced over at her face, and she was just staring up at Robert with a look of intensity in her eyes and almost a snarl on her lips, jerking his cock so hard that she was actually moving his body back and forth.

I looked up at Robert, he was staring down at the two of us, his eyes and mouth reflecting the intensity of his wife's hand jerking his cock.

Robert began to repeat a low breathy, "Oh fuck ... Oh fuck ..."

As a few more groans escaped his throat, Alison brought her free hand up to grip the back of my hair and pushed my head forward, guiding the head of her husband's cock between my lips. She held me in place so that just my lips sealed around the base of the head of his cock. Still frantically pumping his shaft, I realized she was going to jack him off into my mouth. Holding my position on my knees, my hands caressing my breasts, I looked up with just my eyes and they locked with Roberts as he stared down at me.

Although I could see the intense feelings of pleasure in his face, he gave no warning as he began to cum, releasing it all into my mouth as his wife continued to milk him. Typically when a man cums in my mouth, they thrust their hips all the way forward or pull my head all the way in, releasing much of it into my throat as I swallow, but in this position the way Alison was holding my head back, Robert's cock pumped everything right onto my tongue, where I could taste him and struggled to keep up with the amount of his release.

The entire time, he just stared into my eyes, watching me — watching my expression as I so intimately and submissively received his gift. As his orgasm subsided, Alison removed her hand from his shaft, sliding it up on his ass and squeezing in with both of her hands to slide him all the way into my mouth. Trying to relax and adjust as she pushed my head forward, my nose touched the short curly hair above the base of his penis and she just held me there for a few seconds, giving a little shake of my head with her hand.

Pulling my head back with her hand, the head of his cock left my lips with a wet pop. She immediately turned my head and pulled me to her, once again kissing me passionately and driving her tongue between my lips.

After this final kiss, Robert took each of our hands and helped us back to our feet, leaned in to give each of us a gentle kiss and tell us how amazing that was, then walked into the bathroom. Alison turned to me with a smile and said, "I hope you enjoyed all of that as much as we did."

I was honest with her, telling her, "This was not how I expected this evening to go, but yes, it was quite a surprise."

"Was this your first time with a woman?"

"No, but it was only one other time in college. Definitely my first threesome with a woman involved. My goodness, that was something!"

She gave me a caring hug, saying, "I'm glad you enjoyed it. I hoped you would."

I just smiled and said, "I'd better get going, I have a busy day tomorrow and have to leave early to drive home."

"I understand, but you are welcome to stay for the night, just so you know. Robert will be fast asleep, but we can still share a little time together."

Although I perceived nothing but affection and comfort from both of them, I couldn't help but start to feel like I was the third wheel now.

"Thank you. I appreciate the offer, but I really should go."

"No worries … until next time."

I just smiled at her when she said "until next time", not knowing how to respond to that.

Walking out of the bedroom, I found my panties and dress up by the window and slipped them back on. Robert and Alison walked out just as I was getting ready to leave. He was now wearing a robe, but Alison was still parading around in nothing but her high heels.

Robert came over and gave me one last hug and kiss on the cheek, insisting that I get the contract to his office as soon as possible for him to sign. He also assured me that the contract was not contingent on the sex, and hoped they would see me again sometime.

Once back in my room, I drew a nice hot bath, slipped off my dress, high heels, stockings, and panties, then relaxed back in the hot water, reflecting on my evening.

The next morning, I received a call to meet Robert downstairs for breakfast. Already up early, packing up my things and getting ready to check out, it was perfect timing to join him on my way out. I had a several hour drive and wanted to get home early enough in the day to still be productive.

I made my way to the small cafe off the lobby and found Robert and Alison sitting at a cozy table at the back, enjoying a cup of coffee. They both greeted me with a warm hug and kiss, sharing that they wished I would have stayed the night, but understood.

Robert turned the conversation to work, showing me that he was committed to moving forward with our contract, which was really great news for me. I didn't doubt that he was going to sign with us, but it was nice to hear him affirm it.

At one point, Robert got up to go to the restroom, leaving Alison and I alone. She took the opportunity to put her hand on mine, softly caressing it and sincerely telling me how much she enjoyed our intimacy and felt there was a real connection.

She went on to say that she would love to meet up with me again sometime, not necessarily with Robert, perhaps for a fun girl's weekend somewhere. I was flattered, but a little unsure how to respond. I would have never imagined getting a proposition like that from a woman. I simply said "perhaps", and it sounded like it could be fun.

When Robert returned, I expressed my appreciation for their hospitality and the wonderful experience we shared. And like his wife, he also implied we should meet again sometime. I just smiled, replying, "Maybe—sometime—that would be nice," and gave them both a hug before getting underway.

CHAPTER TWENTY-ONE

Sandra Keith

After stopping for gas and getting my GPS all set up, I was on the highway and settled in for my drive. My mind was drifting through all the memories of the night before and trying to make sense of the flood of emotions and feelings I experienced.

I came here expecting something might happen with Robert, I just can't believe his wife joined us. That was just crazy!

The more I thought about Alison, and the way she touched me and kissed me, it took me back to college and brought up so many memories of one of my closest friends, Sandra Keith. All her friends knew her as Sandy. She was a spitfire redhead, always outgoing and passionate about everything she involved herself with. I first met her when I was a freshman, and we pledged together for our sorority. We were paired up for several of the initiations and the things we endured together during the hazing created a quick bond between us.

There was obviously a lot of drinking and stupid pledging we had to do. One particular challenge that we were paired together for was during a party at the sorority house. Several times throughout the night when one of the "bigs" would blow a whistle, all the pledges that were paired together had to immediately strip and exchange all their clothing with their partner in front of everyone. Sandy and I were about the same size so that's probably why they paired us.

We did this four or five times throughout the party in the house, but then at the end of the night, they made each pair of girls do it one last time. We had to run out to the center of the quad yard and do it there before we could run back. That was the time that I specifically remember noticing how Sandy looked at me. It was late and there was just a little bit of light from some of the lamp posts where we stopped. I was wearing Sandy's clothes, and she had on my dress and underwear. She was able to quickly pull the stretchy material dress up over her head and then take off her bra and panties while I was standing there topless and fighting with the buttons on her jean skirt. When I finally got the skirt pushed down around my ankles, and then quickly slid the panties down, I picked them up and looked at her and she was just staring at me with this little smile and look in her eye like she appreciated what she saw. I remember feeling really embarrassed as we handed off the clothes and frantically got dressed before running back across the yard.

Another time, we were all drinking, and the big sisters made us all sit around and play their variation of spin the bottle. I had to kiss several of the girls, and I could tell that they were doing it just because they had to, but the one time I had to kiss Sandy, I could feel that she was into it. Her lips weren't tense, they were soft—and she slipped her tongue into my mouth for a second before breaking off the kiss.

Throughout the next couple years, we were close friends, sorority sisters, and played on the club volleyball team together. I had a boyfriend most of the time through college, and she saw a couple of guys—nothing steady—so I really didn't give much more thought to those initial feelings she gave.

I remember having a few late-night conversations with her, and we would talk about guys and sometimes about sex. At the time I didn't think much about it, but she would ask me if I liked it—if I liked having sex with guys. But then she would ask if the guys went down on me, and if I liked that even more. We were always giggling and making jokes about it, but I think she was trying to feel me out and get some insight into what I liked or was open to.

Honestly, I loved it all. During my college years, it was the time that I became a little wild thing and was quite adventurous with my boyfriends. That was the time that I realized how much I loved having sex. During our senior year, it was a busy time, and we were both feeling the stress of meeting all of our deadlines for graduation, along with playing on the travel volleyball team. It was during that time on a trip to an out-of-state tournament that we shared our experience.

CHAPTER TWENTY-TWO

Cross-court Shot

I think the tournament was in Maryland, and we were there for three days—Friday, Saturday, and Sunday. Our games started early Saturday morning, so we got there the night before, and then the finals were on Sunday.

As usual, Sandy and I were paired up to share a room in the hotel. Both of us were of legal age to drink, but the team policy was no alcohol during team travel. Of course, you know that all the girls followed this rule—not. We were just getting settled into our room and going to get ready to go to dinner with the team when Sandy pulled a big bottle of flavored rum out of her bag.

She was waving it in front of me and said, "Hey—come on—let's do a shot before dinner."

I was shaking my head at her, but replied, "Alright—but just one—we don't want anyone to be suspicious."

After each taking a big shot, we both popped in some breath mints thinking it would hide it and headed down for dinner. It definitely loosened us up but was nothing too bad— it was only one shot. After dinner everyone headed back to their rooms since we had to be up early the next day for the first game. I went to the bathroom and got ready for bed, then came out and climbed into one of the two queen beds in the room. When Sandy came out of the bathroom, she was hugging herself, rubbing her forearms, and exclaimed, "God, it's freezing in here! I'm getting in with you."

Being young college girls, planning ahead was really not one of our strong suits, so neither one of us had anything but t-shirts and cheer shorts to sleep in. It was mid-November, and it was snowing outside, and neither one of us could figure out how to turn the heat up in the room, so it was pretty chilly. I really didn't think much of it when Sandy jumped into bed with me anyway, we would always lay together and talk at night like this.

When she got under the covers, she snuggled right up against me, shivering and laughing, saying she wanted some of my body heat. We laid there, wrapped in each other's arms, and just talked until we fell asleep. The next morning, when I woke up, Sandy was curled in behind me with her arm around my waist. I remember laying there thinking it felt a little awkward, but also kind of nice. When the alarm went off, Sandy woke up and gave me a squeeze and acted as if the way we were embraced in bed was completely normal. Since she didn't act like there was anything weird about it, I went along with it just the same.

We finally dragged ourselves out of bed, gathered our things and headed down to meet the team for breakfast. The team played three games throughout the day, only winning one, so we were eliminated from the finals. Everyone was disappointed, but we still had a lot of fun. Our buses didn't leave until Sunday morning, so we all went out to dinner and then headed back to hang out at the hotel for the evening. Most of us were in a side area of the lobby, where they set up for the complimentary breakfast, but it was empty now. We hung out there until around ten P.M. or so when Sandy leaned over to me and suggested we head up to our room and enjoy some of the rum she brought.

Back in our room, we were sitting at the little round table by the window, taking turns telling stories, sharing embarrassing moments, and after three shots of the rum, we started talking about sex. Sandy asked me all kinds of questions about Mark, my boyfriend at the time, and if he went down on me and if he made me orgasm that way.

"He has—a few times—but he didn't make me cum that way. It's usually just for a few minutes before we have sex," I replied.

I curiously asked back, "Have you ever had an orgasm like that? Like, someone goin' down on you and licking you?"

Sandy got a big smile on her face and said, "Yeah, lots of times. That's one of my favorite things."

Assuming it was with one of the guys she dated, I asked, "Like, did he just do that to you, or was it like before you had sex?"

Smiling again, she replied back, "Who said it was a guy?"

"Oh my God! No way! Really? You let a girl do that to you? Who was it?"

She was giggling at my reaction and then said, "Yeah, I let a girl do it—after all, girls know what they're doing down there. I'm not going to tell you who it was, but you know her."

I was shocked when I heard her telling me this, but I guess not really that surprised. I'd always got the impression from Sandy that there wasn't much she wouldn't do.

"You have to tell me! Come on—who was it?"

"Nope, I don't lick and tell," she laughed.

She got a little serious, and then asked, "So you never had an orgasm from someone going down on you?"

"N ... No."

"And I'm guessing you've never been with a girl either, right?"

"Uh ... No."

We were both quiet for a few seconds, and then Sandy commented, "I remember when you had to kiss me for rush ... and I'm pretty sure it didn't seem like you hated it."

I remember feeling a little embarrassed and nervous when she said that, and then stuttered as I answered, "Well ... No ... I ... I didn't hate it, but that was different, it was just a kiss."

"Have you kissed any other girls since then?"

"No."

"Why not?" she asked with an ornery smile as she leaned forward in her seat.

"I … I don't know, I just … haven't had the opportunity I guess."

"I see. So, if you have the opportunity, you would, right?"

She sat there smiling and staring at me intently, waiting to see what I would say, then I just smiled back at her and said, "Yeah, totally, why not?"

She didn't say anything, but her smile got a little bigger, and then she slowly leaned forward. She stopped, just a couple inches in front of my face—I think trying to see if I was going to pull away—and when I didn't, she closed the gap and pressed her lips against mine. At first, I was a little stiff, but then my eyes fell shut and a slight moan escaped my throat as we began to kiss.

I remember feeling how soft and tender her lips were, and how she nibbled my lower lip. When I began to respond and kiss her back, she slipped her tongue between my lips and started to increase the passion. Feeling so relaxed and easy going with the buzz from the rum, and now feeling aroused from her kiss, I didn't object or say a word when she stood up in front of me and took me by the hand.

Leading me over to the bottom of the bed, she stood facing me, took a step back, and then I watched as she peeled her shirt up over her shoulders and head. Reaching up behind her back, she unclipped her white bra and let it slip forward and down her arms, revealing her breasts to me. They were a little bigger than mine, maybe a C cup, and I couldn't help but notice how cute and hard her pale pink nipples were.

Hooking her thumbs inside of her shorts, she pushed them down over her hips and let them fall from her knees, then brought her hands back up to hook the thin sides of her white bikini panty and pushed them down. Once they were around her ankles with her shorts, she stepped out of them and stood for a few seconds in front of me—naked—letting me look at her. She was a couple of inches taller than me with long thin legs and slim hips. The lips of her pussy were shaved and there was just a small, short patch of hair at the very top.

I remember feeling nervous, and my body trembling as I watched her step forward towards me. She brought her hands up and slipped her fingers up my neck and into the back of my hair, pressing her naked body against me as she once again kissed me passionately for a few seconds.

Breaking the kiss, she hooked the bottom of my shirt with her fingers and slowly began sliding it up. Without a word, I simply raised my arms and let her take the shirt up over my head. I was wearing a white sports bra that she hooked her fingers under and removed next. With my bra tossed over to the side, she brought her fingers in, cocking her head at a slight angle and smiling as she ran her fingertips up my sides and traced them around my breasts until taking them in her palms and caressing them softly.

As she leaned forward, she slid her hands down my sides, replacing them with her lips around my right nipple. Her thumbs hooked in the elastic band at the top of my shorts and then slowly pushed them down over my hips and thighs. Bringing her hands back up, dragging her fingers over the bare skin of my thighs and up to my hip bones, sending a shiver through my body, she pulled my white thong panty down to my knees, exposing my clean shaved mound.

Pulling her lips from my nipple, she lowered herself down to her knees in front of me and finished removing my shorts and panties from my feet. Looking up at me with a slight smile, she placed her hands on the outside of my hips and leaned in and began kissing my thigh and up the front to my hip. Moving slowly, with her lips and her tongue, she kissed her way to the front of my hips and down, ending with a final kiss on the soft lips of my pussy.

Standing back up, she again brought her hands up into the back of my hair, pressing her bare breasts against mine as our lips met once more. Continuing to kiss me, I felt her hands slip down my neck over the outside of my arms and down to my wrists. Her right hand moved inward from my wrist, and I felt her slide her fingers over the front of my hip and then down in between my thighs, her middle finger slipping between the lips of my pussy. Breaking the kiss slightly, an exhaling gasp escaped my lips against hers when I felt the pad of her finger slip over my clit.

She began to gently work her finger in small circles over my clit as I felt her pull my right hand forward by my wrist to touch the front of her hip. Moving her hand to the back of mine, she got it between her legs and pressed my fingers in against her. Filled with nervous excitement, this was the first time I actually touched a woman that way. My hand was still for a few seconds—afraid to move it—but then I slowly began sliding my fingertips up and down the front of her pussy, feeling the soft lips and tracing my finger back up the slit.

I think it was her way of telling me to do more when I felt the finger of her right hand slide down between my legs and she pushed it up inside of me and began flexing it. When I felt her penetrate me, I moaned into her mouth around her tongue that was pressed between my lips and naturally responded by pushing my middle finger between the lips of her pussy.

She was already very wet as I continued to push my finger, and it slid right up inside of her. I started to slowly stroke it in and out and began to notice her returning the moans against my lips. We stood there for a few minutes, passionately kissing, fucking each other's mouths with our tongues as we rubbed and penetrated each other. Both of our free hands had moved to the other's back and were squeezing the cheeks of each other's asses.

Sandy broke the kiss, sliding her fingers from between my legs and taking hold of my wrist to guide me onto the bed with her. She laid me on my back in the middle of the bed, and then moved down between my thighs, laying on her stomach with my knees pushed wide open. I remember holding my head up slightly to watch her, looking up at me with a smile and a look of desire in her eyes as she brought her mouth down and pressed it against my pussy. I let out a low gasp that turned into a long moan as I felt her tongue for the first time press in between my lips to penetrate me, then slide up over my clit and begin to flick back and forth.

"Uuuuhhhh ... God, that feels nice," escaped my lips in a breathy whisper.

Sandy was clearly experienced as she worked her tongue in so many ways I'd never felt before. Everything she said was true—there's nothing like a woman pleasuring another woman this way. She reached up with her hands, still caressing me with her tongue, and began massaging my breasts and pinching and teasing my nipples between her fingers. As soon as her fingers clamped down on my nipples, my body began shuddering under her, a steady moan escaped my throat, and I began to arch my back up from the bed.

It only took a few minutes of this before the most intense orgasm emanated out from my hips and rippled through my body. I couldn't keep from crying out with pleasure, my arms spread wide and gripping at the comforter with my fingers, all while flexing my knees and hips open as wide as I could, rolling my hips against her mouth. Suddenly an intense feeling of overstimulation hit me as her tongue flicked my clit and sent shocks through my body. I quickly brought my hands down to push her head away, turning my body to the side and pulling my knees up in together to curl up, still shuddering with aftershocks from my orgasm. Sandy just laughed as she crawled up my body, running her fingers over my thighs and arms as she curled in behind me.

I could hear her soft voice in my ear, "I told you—wasn't that so much better than a guy?"

Turning my head back towards her, she pulled my arm to slightly roll me to my back. Her hands began gently caressing my breasts, massaging them as I looked at her face and answered, "God … Yeah … that felt so nice."

She just smiled at me for a second, then leaned forward and began to kiss me again—softly. As we laid there kissing, she continued caressing me with her hand, eventually working her fingers back down between my thighs once more, this time with a very soft and caressing touch.

When I began to respond again to her touch, letting out little sighs and whimpers, she broke the kiss and asked, "Are you ready to try more?"

I wasn't quite sure what "more" was, but if it was anything like what I just experienced, I was ready. I answered with only a nod as I licked my lips and swallowed. I watched as she pushed herself up to her knees beside me, looking down at me with a little smile, she swung her knee over top of me, straddling me, facing away. Leaning down forward onto her hands, she began walking her knees back until her open thighs and cute pussy was right over my face.

Oh my God … I've never thought about doing this to another woman. What do I do? What is she going to taste like?

So many nervous thoughts and questions were running through my mind as I felt her lips and tongue once again pressing in between my legs. Already in a heightened sexual state and feeling so aroused, I immediately started responding to her tongue pressing against me. My mouth was open as I was gasping when she pressed her hips back and I felt my lips touch the smooth, soft lips of her pussy.

Nervously, I started to kiss and trace my tongue over her lips. I slid my hands up the back of her thighs until my palms were firmly squeezing and caressing the cheeks of her ass. Sandy had wrapped her arms under my thighs and had my knees pulled up and bent slightly, opening my hips for her when I felt her work two fingers deep up into my pussy and began pumping them in and out.

My body flexed and convulsed for a second as she penetrated me, but then instinctively I began rolling my hips against her hand and tongue. No longer thinking, I was only feeling as I began to actually start kissing the lips of her pussy, and for the first time I thrust my tongue into her. It was such a new sensation for me—the feel and the taste—as I began thrusting it over and over, as deep as I could. Sandy was responding back to me, pressing her hips down against my face, trying to increase the penetration of my tongue. I pulled back slightly and then moved my tongue to her clit where I began to flick and trace circles around it, even occasionally sucking on it with my lips.

We were both now in a frenzy, our mouths trying to out stimulate the other as our bodies were wiggling against each other—broken moans, sighs, and gasps echoing throughout the room. I reached over with my right hand, slipping two of my fingers as deep as I could into her pussy, trying to return the stimulation she was giving me. In a way, it was a constant escalation that she was guiding me as to what to do by demonstrating at first and then waiting for me to follow.

Her next example caught me off guard but felt so incredibly good. I think it was the finger of her other hand, that I felt rubbing the lips of my pussy and around her fingers that were penetrating me. She was getting it nice and wet and then she slid it down all the way to the crack of my ass and began pressing it against my asshole.

At first, I tensed, but then began to trust her and relax when she didn't immediately try to penetrate me, and I came to realize that wasn't her intention—she just wanted to tease me. Every guy I'd been with that touched me there immediately pushed his finger into me, giving little time to adjust, but she was rubbing the flat pad of her finger over my ass, gently pressing just enough to start to open me, but never going further than that. The combination of her tongue on my clit, the fingers she had pulsing in and out of my pussy, and the finger she was rubbing my asshole with felt so incredibly good, and it all translated into me trying to stimulate her just as much. I could feel the imminent building of another orgasm as my body was beginning to tremble and convulse against her stimulation. Not wanting anything to go unmatched, I brought my left hand up over her ass and slipped my thumb down to wet it with her juices, then moved it up to her asshole where I began pressing and rubbing the way she was to me.

I could hear she was close to an orgasm as well, and something in me was determined to give her that pleasure, denying my own until she was ready to join me. We continued to go at each other a few more minutes like this when I suddenly felt her mouth leave me and heard, "Uuughhhh ... You're going to make me cum ... You're going to make me cum!"

When I heard that, I began thrusting my fingers and pressing my tongue in against her with everything I had, also letting myself go, no longer trying to fight back my orgasm.

I heard Sandy begin to cry out as she gave several hard thrusts of her fingers up into me, including letting the one pressing against my ass slip in just an inch or so. When I heard her cries and felt the sudden penetration, my orgasm crashed through my body as well.

Keeping my lips pressed against her, and my tongue pressed between her lips, I moaned and convulsed under the weight of her body as my second orgasm rippled through my being. As I lay there shaking with waves of pleasure, I suddenly felt and tasted a warm sweetness moving over my tongue and against my lips. Though slightly different, I recognized it from myself when I've masturbated or took a man in my mouth right after he's made me cum. Almost in unison, we slowly pulled our fingers from each other and then softly kissed and caressed with our tongues, knowing how sensitive the other felt.

After a few seconds, Sandy pushed up off of my body and turned around to lay with me, holding each other in our arms. I immediately realized one of the benefits of making love to a woman. After sex another woman doesn't want to run off or fall asleep, she wants to continue to embrace in the moment—and it felt really nice.

We fell asleep like that, our naked bodies intertwined, our thighs pressed in between each other's. The next morning when we woke up, we were still lying against each other, in a similar position. A new day, with a new perspective, the rum had worn off and I felt many emotions thinking back about what we did. We didn't have time to talk about anything then, we had to go downstairs to meet the team for the bus. We had to be careful, but on the bus, we were able to talk, and I was honest with her—and my feelings—or so I thought.

I didn't deny how incredible it was—and also how much I was into it and truly enjoyed it—but Sandy understood when I expressed to her that I like guys, and I really like sex with guys. We never hooked up again like that, probably because there wasn't a perfect opportunity like that night, but we stayed close friends through graduation. The last I heard was Sandy was openly gay and living happily with a partner in Colorado.

I guess I've never really let myself remember that night or embrace those feelings with a woman until this unexpected meeting with Robert and his wife. I'd put it out of my mind and forgotten how incredibly passionate that night was.

CHAPTER TWENTY-THREE

Suppressed and Awakened

After a few days, life had returned to normal, falling back into the grind of work and family, but every once in a while, something would remind me, or I would catch myself daydreaming and reminiscing.

I found myself being more aware of some of the women around me, and how they interacted with me. Looking at women I've known for years and thinking, *I wonder if she's ever been with a woman?*

I wasn't becoming obsessed with it by any means, but the seeds had definitely been planted—and I was thinking about it at times. Trying to get my head around what I was desiring, what I was craving, I compared it with thoughts I'd had about men and realized it was something totally different.

When I desired a man, when I felt the need to be with a man, I craved his masculinity. I wanted to be submissive to him, feel his power, his aggressiveness, his control. I wanted to feel him penetrating me and using my body, pleasuring himself with me. Taking out his sexual frustration on me and being that outlet for him. I received pleasure from being his pleasure, and I loved that.

But the feelings of desire to be with a woman were almost the complete opposite. It was the desire to feel comforted and pampered and caressed. That was what I felt with both Sandra and Alison—they cared about my pleasure and comfort and gave it to me in such a feminine way. I wasn't craving going down on them the way I do with a man, it wasn't about the physical act as much, it was the emotional connection with a woman.

The most common time I found myself slipping away to these thoughts was if I had time to relax in a hot bubble bath. Dimming the lights, lighting a few candles, and just relaxing in the hot water, it was easy to let my mind drift back to that night with Sandy. It felt so sensual and relaxing, my fingers slipping over my body in the soapy water, caressing my breasts and teasing my nipples, then letting my fingers slide down over my stomach between my thighs. I'd pull my feet in and open my hips as wide as I could in the tub, gently letting the pad of my middle finger slip between my lips and flutter it back and forth over my clit, letting myself imagine it's a woman's tongue pleasuring me.

CHAPTER TWENTY-FOUR

My Husband's Fantasy, My Excuse

It had been about six months or so since my encounter with Robert and Alison, and though I still let my mind occasionally visit those experiences, for the most part I'd put those thoughts and fantasies on a shelf.

It was a Friday night after a long and busy week for both me and my husband and we decided to enjoy a low-key night at home, curl up on the couch, and watch a movie. It wasn't my first choice, but we ended up watching Wild Things with Denise Richards, Neve Campbell, and Matt Dillon. To my surprise, at one point in the movie, the three stars enjoyed a threesome. When the scene started to unfold and I realized what was going to happen, out of curiosity I started paying closer attention to my husband's expressions and body language.

He likes It ... He likes it a lot, I thought to myself as I watched him intently enjoy the scene and adjust his hips a little bit.

Playfully, I slid my hand over his thigh and onto his crotch where I found he was starting to get semi-erect, then looked at him and smiled, asking, "Does that excite you?"

I wasn't completely naive when I asked that, since there had been times in the past where jokes were made and I had a pretty good idea that he was aroused by the thought of being with two women, but it wasn't something I gave much thought to then.

Tensing up slightly and looking a little nervous, he answered, "I mean ... I suppose so—yeah, it's hot. Pretty sure all guys would love that—at least the straight ones," he added, trying to joke.

"Hmmm ..." was all I responded with, playing with him and letting him squirm a little.

But then I let him off the hook, "I'm just messing with you, you're not in trouble—I agree, I think it's pretty hot too."

When I said that his eyes got bigger and his body language changed as he asked, "Are you being serious? You actually think that's hot too—two women with one guy?"

"Yeah, I do. Why? You think you could handle me and another woman?" I said teasingly as I gave him a squeeze through the front of his pants.

"Handle it? I was thinking it would take more than two of you to handle me," he joked, laying it on thick.

I laughed, but then asked him a little more directly, "But seriously, is that something you would like? Is that a fantasy you have—your wife and another woman ... all over you ... pleasuring you ... pleasuring each other?"

I continued to slowly stroke him down the leg of his pants, now fully erect as I could see him no doubt imagining what I just described. I could tell he was still guarded and afraid to answer honestly, maybe thinking I was trying to trick him into saying something. But I wasn't, I truly wanted to know. Trying to reassure him and get him to open up, I added, "Tell me—I really do want to know—does that excite you?"

"What if I said it did?"

I squeezed a little tighter as I stroked his shaft through the material of his pants, looking in his eyes and answering, "Then I'd want to know more. I'd like to hear what you fantasize about. I'd like to know what you imagine the three of us doing. Tell me."

I took my hand from between his legs only long enough to turn the TV off, then brought it back to open the front of his pants. Reaching inside, I pulled him free and began moving my hand up and down his shaft, each time running my thumb over the tip to smear his pre-cum to my palm.

Looking back up at him again I reiterated, "Tell me what you imagine us doing."

He swallowed and took a few breaths, then started to open up, "I'd love to watch you both kiss. Watch you undress each other. I imagine you squeezing each other's tits, kissing them and sucking on them."

I was happy he was starting to talk, but I could tell this was all tame and reserved, so I encouraged him a little. Knowing the secret to getting a man to open up—it's like a truth serum. I dropped my head down and took him into my mouth for a few seconds, bobbing up and down as I stroked him with my hand, then sat back up and looked at him, asking, "Would you want us to go down on you at the same time? Take turns with you—with our lips?"

I could see in his expression that just the thought of it excited him, but I wanted to hear him say it. I leaned forward again, taking the head of his penis between my lips and sucking it for a few seconds, then lifted off of him just long enough to ask, "Well? One of us sucks like this, while the other licks and sucks at your balls maybe?"

Immediately I dropped my mouth back down over him and started to slide most of his length all the way in and out of my lips as I heard him answer through his heavy breathing, "Yeah, just like that."

I worked him a little more intensely with my hand and mouth, then came up just long enough to ask, "Would you want to watch us go down on each other?"

Dropping my mouth back down over him, he let out a low moan and then answered, "That would be fucking incredible to see."

I could tell I was starting to get him into a good place to fantasize with me and get him to share. I worked him feverishly for another minute or so with my hand and mouth, then stood up in front of him and hastily pulled my t-shirt up over my head and threw it to the side. Just as quickly, I pushed the black leggings down my legs and kicked them off. Now completely naked, I climbed back onto the couch to straddle him, reaching down with my right hand to guide his penetration, I lowered my hips all the way down, pushing my knees open wide and taking every inch of him.

He slid his hands up the outside of my thighs, to my hips, and then around to caress the cheeks of my ass as I began slowly grinding into him. He was looking up at me with passion and desire in his eyes, and I'll admit I hadn't seen that from him in quite a while. It was nice. Clearly, I sparked something deep inside of him with my questions and I wanted to know more.

"Mmmmm .... So, tell me ... would you want to get behind me ... Fuck me while I go down on her?"

"Oh God ... I'd fuck you so hard if you were doing that," he answered intensely as he the thrust his hips upward into me.

"And what about her? Would you fuck her just as hard if she was going down on me?"

Even though he was so intensely aroused, and I was continuing to grind my hips into him, I could see the hesitation in his eyes, not knowing if he could admit he wanted to fuck another woman. I let him off the hook as I answered for him, "I'd want you to. I'd want you to make her moan and cry out as I held her head between my legs, looking up at you and sharing our connection."

He didn't answer but just nodded his head in agreement as he began the groan and moved one of his hands up to squeeze my breasts. I transitioned from grinding my hips to a full bounce on his lap, coming down hard, trying to drive him as deep into me as I could. His mouth was gaped open now as he dropped his head back to relax and let me do all the work. As he watched me, I continued flexing my thighs to raise and lower my body on him and I brought my hands up to squeeze my breasts together, mauling myself and pinching and twisting my nipples for both of our enjoyment.

It didn't take long before I had myself on the edge of an orgasm. Riding him this way always hit just the right spots. Squeezing my breasts in together once more, I looked deep into his eyes and told him I was going to cum.

"Cum with me … I'm gonna cum … Cum with me," just escaped my lips as my mouth dropped open and I let out a long gasp and cry of pleasure.

I continued to watch his face, stare into his eyes, as my body shuddered in front of him, and enjoyed the expression on his face as I felt his erection throbbing inside of me, releasing. Falling forward, I pressed my lips into his and we shared a passionate kiss. A kiss like we used to share, in the beginning. It was wonderful. The feeling of his arms wrapped around me, one hand gripping my side and the other up under my hair, squeezing my naked body against him. I could feel that he still loved me, still desired me. I knew what I wanted to give him now.

CHAPTER TWENTY-FIVE

Planning by the Pool

Every year, usually in August, we try to get away and unplug a little with a trip to the beach. That year I decided to use the opportunity to plan something special during our trip. The resort hotel that I chose in Miami was a little outside our normal destination area, and a little more taxing on the budget, but it would be well worth it. Truth is, I didn't choose it. It was the destination of convenience to put my plan in motion.

After that insightful night on the couch, sharing the thoughts of my husband's fantasies for a threesome, I knew I wanted to make that happen for him. The problem I had was trying to figure out how, where, and most importantly, with whom? It was going to be a very intimate night, and I was struggling with figuring out how to meet the right woman. There was no way I could leave it up to a chance meeting. It wasn't something I could involve one of my friends. I didn't want any of them to know. And even if I found someone online that seemed like a possibility, there were so many concerns about safety, trust, and chemistry.

When I first had the thought of giving my husband this experience it seemed so simple, but when I actually started to try and plan it, it became frustrating and appeared like I wasn't going to be able to make it happen.

If only I could find someone like Alison … Wait … That's it!

Although we didn't keep in close touch, Alison and I did become friends on Facebook, so I messaged her.

```
Hi beautiful, I hope everything is well in
your world! I have a favor to ask, something
very intimate that I feel like you're the
only one I could possibly consider. That
night with you and Robert was incredibly
erotic, and memorable, and I've reminisced
many times. I hope you felt the same. I've
never shared any of that with my husband,
but since then I've learned that it's always
been one of his fantasies to experience a
night like that. Sooo … The thing I want to
```

```
ask  you  is  would  you  be  interested  in
joining  us  one  evening,  to  help  me  give  him
a  night  like  that?  Please  feel  no  pressure,
I  totally  understand  if  it's  not  something
you  can  do.  I  just  really  want  to  give  him
this  and  I  can't  imagine  anyone  more  perfect
than  you  to  share  it  with.  I  hope  to  hear
back  soon,  take  care!
```

It wasn't until the next day that I received a response. I remembered feeling nervous excitement when I first sent the message, but then when I saw she responded, I was surprised at how anxious I felt.

```
Hey  you!  YES!!!  I'm  flattered  that  you
asked,  and  I  would  love  to.  How  do  you  want
to  do  this?
```

Oh my God, I can't believe this is actually going to happen!

Over the next few days, we messaged back and forth and worked out all the details. The hotel we were staying at in Miami is one of the new properties that Robert's company acquired, and Alison was going to be in town that weekend and staying there. She told me that Robert was not going to be with her on that trip, but he was fully aware and supportive. All of this was so exciting, I could barely stand the anticipation, but it was a couple months away, so I had to put it on a shelf.

When the date finally arrived, I had to actually work at staying calm and not making my husband suspicious. We were at the resort for a few days before Alison arrived, enjoying all the amenities and soaking up the sun, but the best was yet to come. Saturday morning, I received a text from Alison, saying she had just arrived, was up in her room, and would love to see me before the evening. The timing was perfect since my husband was going to be gone all morning playing golf. Both of us, having the same thought, decided to meet up and enjoy a little time at the pool. I slipped on one of my favorite little suits, a brown string bikini with adjustable panels that allow to cover or show as much as I dare. The other thing so sexy about this bikini is that when my tan gets darker, like it is now, at a glance it almost looks like I'm naked. I slipped a cream-colored sheer cover-up over top, selected a pair of high-heeled wedge sandals, grabbed my bag, and headed down.

Alison hadn't come down yet, so I stood by the statue in the lobby where we planned to meet, feeling a little exposed, but enjoyed the looks from people passing and taking notice of my skimpy bikini under my sheer cover-up. Two men even took the opportunity to stop and sit on a bench just off to my side and very obviously take the time to appreciate my outfit. Never one to waste an opportunity to flirt or tease, I made sure to turn and position myself to afford them every angle, even bending at the waist with my behind in their direction as I set my bag down.

After a few minutes, Alison appeared from the elevators and excitedly hurried over to me, embracing me in a warm hug, followed by a kiss on the lips that clearly said we were more than friends. Alison was wearing a red string bikini that was more string than material with a tan mesh cover-up that really hid nothing. I glanced over at my admirers and noticed we had their undivided attention. Hand in hand, we headed off to the pool, and I couldn't resist making eye contact with them, giving a knowing smile as we walked by.

We laid by the pool, enjoyed a few fruity drinks, and for the first time actually talked. Despite how intimately involved I'd been with Alison, I really knew very little about her. Apparently, she met Robert not long out of college, after graduating with a degree in interior design. A firm she was working with was hired to reimagine one of Robert's properties and she caught his eye during a presentation. Although she doesn't have to, she said she enjoys working with Robert and oversees much of the creative decor for several of their properties. That's why she was at this property for the next couple of days.

Out of curiosity, I couldn't help but inquire about their arrangement and how they openly see other people. She admittedly agreed that typical relationships like this don't last, but said Robert was wonderful and they do love each other. She said the times with other people were purely for fun—just sex with friends—and she and Robert share everything about the experiences and love that they can do that.

After a short pause, I looked over at her and asked, "So, you told Robert about meeting me here with my husband?"

"Yeah."

"And when you get home, you'll tell him everything that happened?"

"Everything."

"And he doesn't mind at all hearing that?" I asked.

With a smile, she replied, "Not only does he not mind, but he also loves hearing it. It drives him nuts, but in a good way.

A lot of the time, the men I'm with are at his encouragement. If I come back from a trip, and don't have a story, he's actually disappointed."

She continued, "So when you messaged me with this idea, he was very excited for me to come do it with you. His exact words were, 'Oh, fuck yeah, you've got to do it'."

We talked more about the plan for the evening, and I reiterated that my husband had no idea that I knew her, or about anything that had happened. She just smiled and confirmed, "Don't worry, it'll just be a once-in-a-lifetime chance meeting at a bar on vacation. This is going to be so fun!"

I could tell she was genuinely excited, and not just because of the sex, but for the whole scene we had elaborately planned to play out. I heard my phone "beep", and it was a text from my husband letting me know he was on his way back. I finished the last of my drink and told her, "I need to get back to the room and get ready. My husband booked a speedboat sightseeing tour for the afternoon, and then we'll be back for dinner, drinks, and ..."

We both smiled at each other, stood up and hugged, and I made my way back towards the hotel. Before I entered the hotel, I looked back over and could see Alison already in the pool and talking with two very muscular hot young guys that were staring at us the entire morning. I just smiled to myself and shook my head, thinking, *I hope she saves some energy for tonight.*

Back in my room, I just finished freshening up when I heard the door unlocking. I decided to keep my bikini on for the boat ride but replaced the sheer cover-up with a little more concealing short white strapless bodycon dress.

After the morning at the pool, and a couple of drinks, I was feeling wonderfully relaxed and excited about the day. When my husband walked in, I gave him a playful look and walked over, wrapping my arms up around his neck, and giving him a passionate kiss.

"Mmmm … What's got into you?" he asked after I broke away from the kiss.

"Just feeling relaxed and enjoying this little getaway with you."

He dropped his hands down, cupping the cheeks of my ass and squeezing my hips in against him as he initiated another kiss, this time driving his tongue into my mouth. After a minute or so of kissing and letting him grope me, I pushed him away, saying, "Alright … save it for later, we'll have plenty of time this evening. We don't want to be late for your boat ride."

"Ahhh … How about just a quickie?" he pleaded as he pulled the hem of my dress up around my waist.

Normally, I would have obliged, but I wanted to keep him worked up and ready for the evening ahead. I dropped my hand down to the front of his shorts and squeezed him through the material, pleasantly surprised at how hard he was.

"No, not yet—I think I want to keep you this way all day, and then I'll take care of you tonight."

"God, you're such a tease—and I love it," he added with a smile.

I gave a little smile back as I stepped away, smoothing my dress back down, thinking to myself how happy it made me seeing him happy and feeling the desire from him. Little did he know the night I had planned for him.

The speed boat tour he booked was all his idea, but I have to be honest, it was so much more fun than I expected—and it was big! I was expecting a speedboat with a few people on it, but there were like twenty people on this huge boat. While we stood in line to get on the boat, I noticed several of the other women wearing swimsuits with wrap skirts, so I pulled the top of my dress down and bunched it around my waist to make it into a skirt. When my husband looked back at me, he did a double take and commented with a smile, "That looks better."

"It's not too revealing?" I asked playfully since my bikini top was a lot skimpier than everyone else's.

"I don't think so," he eagerly answered with a big smile.

Most of the people getting on the boat were older couples, and I did notice many of the husbands giving me an appreciative look. During the boat ride, on more than one occasion, I felt like I was going to slip out of the top as the boat bounced along some of the bigger waves. My husband and a few of the men around me enjoyed the show. It was obvious that as we walked back to the car it was still on my husband's mind enough to comment about it, telling me he was hoping for a little flash. Wanting to continue teasing him, just before we got in the car, I called out to him and when he looked up, I pulled the material covering my breasts off to each side, giving him a playful tease. He just laughed and commented "Now that's what I was waiting for."

I knew I was keeping him in the place I wanted by the constant comments and wandering, groping hands as we made our way back to our room.

CHAPTER TWENTY-SIX

A Night He Will Never Forget

My husband was in the bathroom getting a shower as I unpacked my outfit for the evening. The dress was a coral-colored, deep cut wrap that fell a couple inches above mid-thigh. The hem was very short and loose, making it the perfect sexy dress for an evening of dancing and teasing. The only other things I selected were a pair of the skimpiest sheer beige g-string panties I had and a pair of four-inch, high-heeled, strappy beige sandals. As soon as my husband came out, I pushed past him, fighting off his groping advances and pressing his naked self against me as I laughed, telling him to let me go get ready.

With the final spritz of perfume, I stood in front of the mirror checking myself out, feeling incredibly sexy and excited. I walked out of the bathroom and my husband was making himself a drink over at the mini bar, dressed in a baby blue button-up shirt and a pair of tan slacks with brown flip flops. When he turned and looked at me, his expression told me that he was quite pleased with what he saw, followed by, "Wow! You look hot!"

"You look pretty good yourself. While you're there, why don't you make me one of those too."

He handed me my glass and raised his for a toast, saying, "Here's to getting away from life, and to my beautiful wife."

After thinking how sweet that was, I added, "And here's to my handsome husband, and making all of his fantasies come true."

"Ooooh, I like the sound of that," he responded as we downed our drinks.

You have no idea what's in store for you, I thought to myself as I smiled at him, setting my glass down.

He stepped forward and slipped his hands around my waist, pulling me in as he leaned down to kiss me. I could feel the desire in his kiss, and in his hands as they slid down over my ass and worked their way under the back hem of my dress, squeezing my bare cheeks in his palms.

Pulling back from the kiss, he whispered to me, "Mmm, you're going to make me wait until after dinner for any fun, aren't you?"

I playfully slipped my hand down between our bodies and began to stroke his semi-erect penis down the leg of his trousers through the material, teasing back, "Aww ... What's the matter? You can't wait that long? Do you need something to hold you over?"

"Yeah, just a little somethin'," he pouted back.

I found the zipper to his pants and pushed it down, then slipped my hand inside and wrapped my fingers around his now erect shaft and began caressing it, stroking and squeezing it down against his thigh.

"How's that? Does that help?"

Through little moans and grunts, he answered, "Yeah, that helps. But you know what would really help? Your lips wrapped around it."

I smiled at him, pulled my hand out of his pants, paused for just a second, then stooped down in front of him. Bringing my fingers up to the front of his pants, staring up into his eyes and seeing the lustful desire he was looking down at me with, I abruptly pushed his zipper up. Quickly standing back up and stepping away, I just giggled and said, "After dinner," then turned and walked toward the door.

I heard him behind me playfully groaning and then following me out of the room and down the hallway. When he caught up to me in the hallway, he just looked at me shaking his head and said, "Such a tease."

We enjoyed a wonderful dinner, and I made sure to continue keeping him on the edge with a little footsie under the table throughout. We both were on our third cocktail and feeling pretty good. That's when I noticed Alison walk in— right on time—and make her way over to the bar. She was wearing a sexy white spaghetti strap backless mini dress that was cut with a deep V between her breasts and an overall flaring A-line cut. Her hemline fell at her upper thigh and white high-heeled sandals that tied up around her ankle completed the outfit. She turned quite a few heads as she walked into the room and made her way over to climb up onto a stool between two older men sitting at the bar. She glanced in my direction and flashed a little smile before turning her back to me. Over the next twenty minutes or so, my husband and I enjoyed another cocktail and relaxed, people watching and talking about everyone around us. Alison was still at the bar, laughing and chatting with the two men on either side of her, no doubt flirting with both of them and getting them to buy her drinks. Both of us were just waiting for the DJ to start so we could make our way to the dance floor where we planned to start our evening.

When the lights dimmed and the music started thumping, I looked over at my husband as I swayed in my seat, "I want to dance. You comin' with me?"

He just smiled, shaking his head "no" and said, "You go—have fun—I'll just watch you."

That was the response I expected. He always needs a few more drinks before I can drag him out to the dance floor, but that was fine tonight, I was going to have another dance partner. Taking my drink in hand, I danced my way through the bar and onto the dance floor. There were a few couples dancing, but mostly groups of girls. About halfway through the first song, I was in the middle of the floor surrounded by people when I felt someone brush against me from behind. Looking back over my shoulder I realized my accomplice had arrived.

We stayed in character, slowly building our interactions and trying to present a natural creation of our connection as my husband looked on from the corner. After about twenty minutes or so of dancing, whispering in each other's ears and laughing as we appeared to grow closer and closer, I decided it was time to introduce my husband. Both needing a refill on our drinks, I grabbed Alison by the hand and led her over to where my husband was seated.

"Honey, I want you to meet my new friend, Ali," I yelled to him over the music as we approached the table, both playfully laughing and smiling at my husband.

I knew my husband well enough to recognize the expression on his face, and the way his eyes betrayed him scanning up and down her body. He was impressed with her. After the initial introductions and pleasantries, I went on to tell my husband that she was staying at the hotel alone for work and how we hit it off and just felt a connection. We sent my husband up to the bar to get us another round of drinks while we sat and colluded. We were sitting on the two end stools by the table, my back to the bar and Alison close in front of me. I kept seeing Alison's eyes dart over to the bar and back, so I asked her, "Is he watching us?"

"Yes, and he has this big grin on his face. How about I give him something to look at?"

I looked at her with a questioning smile and then watched as she leaned forward and put her hand on my knee, and then slowly caressed the top of my thigh between my knee and the hem of my dress. Stealing a glance over my shoulder, she smiled at me and then said, "That got his attention. You should see him straining his neck to try to see where my hand is going."

We giggled and continued to make our plans as she moved her hand up and down my thigh.

"Here he comes with our drinks," Alison said as she sat back up and moved her hand away.

"Here you go ladies. I hope you don't mind; I had the bartender make them doubles," he proudly stated looking at us for our reaction.

Alison smiled and quickly quipped, "Mmm, I think he's trying to get lucky."

My husband just laughed and shrugged his shoulders. Just then, the DJ started playing *Brick House,* and feeling the groove, Alison and I headed back to the dance floor giggling hand in hand. I glanced back at my husband as we moved away, and he gave me a raised eyebrow look of approval.

Back on the dance floor, the two of us started dancing closer and closer, bumping and grinding and putting on a show for my husband. At one point, Alison was behind me with her free hand around my waist as she ground into my body from behind.

The bar lights were a little lower now and the atmosphere had turned toward a party vibe with the DJ controlling the mood. The dance floor was starting to get pretty crowded and a lot of times we were hidden from my husband's view by the bodies moving around us. That's when the DJ brought it down and started to play a slow song.

Alison just gave me an ornery look and then headed off in my husband's direction, leaving me standing on the dance floor alone. I watched as she grabbed him by the hand. He only put up a brief fight before she was able to get him out of his seat. After she brought him to the dance floor, I assumed she was bringing him to me, but she actually joined us and the three of us started to sway to the slow beat.

We were all feeling our drinks at this point, and Alison started talking to my husband about me, "Your wife is so beautiful! You're a very lucky man."

"Yes, I know, I am," he answered, looking at me lovingly.

Up to this point, we were standing in a close triangle swaying together, but then Alison moved me in between her and my husband, with my back to him and facing her. He immediately dropped his hands down to my hips and I felt his body press in against me. Alison moved in closer, also putting her hands down at my waist. I could tell she was running her fingers over my body through my thin dress but also running them over my husband's hands as he held me tight.

She was staring at me, into my eyes with an intense lustful look when out of nowhere she brought her body all the way in against me and pressed her lips into mine.

I let my eyes drop shut and began passionately returning her kiss, our tongues dancing between our lips as we both surrendered.

When we first began to kiss, I heard "Oh fuck" escape my husband's lips by my ear and then felt the unmistakable press of his erection against my ass as he started to grind into me. The kiss only lasted about ten seconds, and then Alison stepped back, giving me an ornery smile and throwing her arms up in the air as she started seductively dancing in front of us. She was swaying seductively and looking back and forth between my face and my husband's.

My husband continued to grind himself into me from behind for the remainder of the song, then as it ended, he put his lips by my ear and asked, "Were you okay with that?"

I turned to face him, putting my arms up around his neck, I looked at him with a smile and said, "Yeah … Are you okay with it?"

"Uhhhh, yeah!" he said with a sarcastic excitement.

"Good, because I have a feeling it's going to go further," I told him and then gave him a quick kiss on the lips before pushing away to dance with Alison again.

Peeking back over my shoulder at him with a naughty smile, he was just staring at us with this look of disbelief. After a few minutes of moving to the music, bumping and grinding with Alison, I realized I had been so caught up in our act that

I hadn't paid much attention to anyone around us. As we continued to dance, I started looking around the room. My husband was off to the side of the dance floor leaning against the wall in a dark area, sipping his drink with a smile on his face, enjoying our show. But he wasn't the only one watching, as I scanned the room, at least four or five other guys seemed to be fixated on our gyrating interactions. Alison was dancing as if there was no one else around and we were the only two on the dance floor, without a care for what anyone saw or thought. Not one to be self-conscious, I smiled to myself at the attention we were garnering as I moved in close and put my hands up around her neck. Her hands immediately slid onto my waist and began alternating, moving up and down over the outside of my hips in time with the music as we swayed and stared into each other's eyes.

It's time, I thought to myself as I leaned in and whispered in her ear. With an agreeing nod, I took her hand, and we made our way off the dance floor and over to my husband.

"You just standing off to the side enjoying the show, huh?" I asked playfully.

Alison chimed in, "So you like to watch, don't you?"

A little smile formed on his lips and before he could answer, I interjected, "Yeah ... He likes to watch."

At this point I could tell he didn't know how to respond as I turned and looked at Alison with a smile.

"Well, if that's the case, why don't we go somewhere and give him something to watch?" Alison suggested.

Looking back at my husband, I could tell he was in complete shock at what was unfolding right in front of him.

After a couple seconds of silence, just enjoying his disbelief, Alison took my hand, I grabbed my husband's, and she said, "Come on ... Let's go ... Let's get out of here."

Just as we approached the elevators, a few people were getting on one as the doors opened to the second and it emptied. Alison quickly diverted us to the empty elevator and pushed the button for the top floor. My husband was standing in the center of the back and before the doors even closed, Alison turned my body to face her as she backed herself up against him. Pulling my body into hers, she sandwiched herself between us as we started to passionately kiss. I could tell my husband was nervous but incredibly excited, so I gave him some encouragement to let him know it was okay to join in our embrace. Alison was passionately kissing me, one of her hands slipping into my hair as the other found its way inside the top of my dress to caress my bare breast. I reached back with my hands to find my husband's and pull them forward, placing them on Alison's hips. That was all he needed in his intoxicated state, immediately beginning to move his fingers up and down to feel her body through her thin white dress.

The "ding" of the elevator interrupted our embrace. The doors opened and without saying any words, we all shuffled out and followed Alison to the door of her suite. Once inside, Alison took the lead, showing us through the living area and into the master bedroom where she positioned my husband in a chair in the corner and playfully told him, "You just get to watch right now."

The look on his face was so cute and telling, like a kid in a massive candy store for the first time, barely able to contain his excitement. Within seconds, Alison and I were lost in an embrace, passionately kissing and undressing each other as we stood at the bottom of the bed in front of my husband. Once her dress was off, she was standing completely naked in only her white high heels. My dress joined hers on the floor, leaving me in nothing but my beige high-heeled sandals and sheer g-string panty.

It felt so sensual, our naked breasts pressed against each other as our tongues danced between our lips and our hands roamed up and down each other's back. Never breaking the kiss, Alison turned her body slightly, enough to slide her hand to the front of my hips and slip her delicate fingers inside the front of my panties. My sigh of pleasure escaped around her tongue as I felt her finger slip gently between the lips of my pussy. My body began to twitch and tremble as she expertly worked the pad of her finger over my clit, now slippery with my juices. She abruptly pulled her hand away and stepped back, glancing over at my husband with a smile, she turned her attention back and led me over to the bed.

As I climbed onto the bed, she hooked her fingers into the thin band of my panties and slipped them down my legs and over my high heels, then playfully tossed them over at my husband. I turned to lie down on my back in the center of the bed. Alison leaned down to briefly kiss my breasts and suck each of my nipples between her lips, giving a playful tease with her teeth before swinging her leg over my body to position us for a "69".

I pulled my knees up and pushed them out, opening my hips at the same time as Alison pushed her knees out and lowered herself to my tongue. Over the next few minutes, the room was filled with the escalating sound of muffled moans through wet licking. Occasionally, I could hear Alison speaking to my husband, one time telling him, "Your wife's pussy is so sweet—come taste it."

I continued flicking my tongue aggressively back and forth over her clit as I heard movement from my husband's chair to the bottom of the bed. Feeling the roughness of his stubble against my thigh, I knew it was now his tongue pressing into me as she encouraged him.

"That's it—taste how sweet she is. Finger her while you lick her."

I let out a low moan as I felt my husband's thicker fingers slip up into me as he continued to lick and suck at my sensitive clit. Wanting to pass what I was feeling on to her, I brought my hand up and worked two of my fingers deep into Alison's pussy and began to pulse them in and out. I could hear the effect it had in her breathing and broken sentences as she spoke to my husband. I too was getting close to an orgasm with my husband thrusting his fingers deep into me. Out of nowhere, my first orgasm rippled through my body as I let out a moan and drove my fingers deep into Alison. Pinned down by Alison's body, and with no way to stop him, my husband continued fingering me with his aggressive excitement past my normal point of pleasure and into an overstimulated frenzy as I squirmed and convulsed to no avail. A steady cry was escaping my throat as I felt the two of them feeding on my response.

I could tell Alison enjoyed pushing my limits, but she finally stopped my husband and moved from on top of my body. I laid there panting and writhing on the bed for a few seconds as my body twitched and I regained my composure. Lifting my head, I saw my husband kneeling at the bottom of the bed, his lips glistening with my wetness and the look of disbelief and intense arousal in his eyes. Alison leaned down by my ear and whispered, "I think we teased him enough, let's give him a little pleasure."

With a smile and a nod, I pushed myself up and crawled to the edge of the bed, following Alison down to the bottom where we stood my husband up and then worked together to undress him. I just smiled at him as I unbuttoned the front of his shirt while Alison worked on his belt and lowered his pants. Springing free, I don't think his erection could have been any harder. I could tell she was tempted to take hold of it, but Alison refrained as we let him stand there naked in front of us with his pants around his ankles. Playfully pushing him back onto the bed, we removed his pants, then took our positions at the bottom of the bed, kneeling on each side of his hips. Alison lowered her lips and began kissing the inside of his thigh as I leaned forward and did the same over his stomach. He was propping himself up on his elbows, just staring down at us with intense anticipation as he watched us work our way closer to his erection, standing proudly and pulsing in the air. His head dropped back, and a groan escaped his throat as simultaneously Alison's lips kissed one of his shaved testicles and my lips pressed and slid up the top of his shaft.

His groans only intensified as Alison began sucking and flicking her tongue while my mouth moved over the tip and my lips sealed around the head and sucked him in. We spent the next few minutes taking turns bobbing and sucking, alternating between kissing each other and up and down the shaft of his penis. I wrapped my fingers around the base of his shaft and squeezed with short strokes, pumping him into

Alison's mouth while she bobbed up and down. Continuing to hold him this way, I moved my lips up to his and gave him a passionate kiss, then told him seductively, "We're going to fuck you now."

He didn't say anything, just nodded his head and watched. Alison pushed herself up to her knees, her lips leaving my husband's cock with a wet pop. She positioned herself just to his side, her knees spread as wide as her shoulders as her right hand slipped between her legs to pleasure herself for their mutual enjoyment. I swung my leg over top of my husband's hips and reached down, taking his shaft in my hand, I lowered myself onto him. With a long pleasurable gasp, I settled my hips all the way down and began grinding with a rolling motion. I reached down and grabbed his hand resting on my thigh and brought it up to my left breast. Following my lead, Alison took his right hand and brought it up to her breast as well. He was pulsing his hips up into me as his hands squeezed and mauled our breasts, pinching and twisting our nipples while I rode him, and Alison fingered herself. Leaning over, Alison met me halfway and we began to kiss again, both for our pleasure and putting on a show for my husband.

Breaking the kiss, I looked back at my husband and gave a few hard bounces before pushing myself up off of him and kneeling beside him. Looking over at Alison, I nodded and motioned with my eyes for her to take my place. I watched the look on my husband's face, his expression portraying disbelief that this was even happening, as Alison moved over top of him and guided his penis into her. Bracing herself with her hands on his chest, she began bouncing her hips on him, fucking him for the first time, right in front of me. A swell of emotions went through me. I didn't feel jealousy, but there was a sense of need to feel connected to him and share this moment I was giving him. Leaning down, I passionately kissed him, whispering, "I love you," and assuring him I wanted to make his fantasies come true.

Pushing back up, Alison had slowed her pace slightly but was now flexing her thighs to raise and lower her hips on him as she squeezed her breasts in a teasing way for him. Abruptly stopping, she pushed back and slid down his legs, dropping her lips around his glistening shaft and taking him deep into her mouth, sucking and moaning with her eyes closed. Her feet were on the floor as she leaned over the bottom of the bed between his legs, slowly working him with her mouth, taking every inch of him. I watched, mesmerized for a few minutes as I let my hand drop between my legs to rub myself, watching every inch of my husband's shaft disappearing between Alison's lips.

When Alison opened her eyes and looked up at me, I instructed her to stay in that position, then looked at my husband and told him to get behind her. As he slid to the side of the bed and walked around behind her, I took his place, spreading my legs wide and sliding down to put myself right in front of her mouth. She looked into my eyes, with a smile, as she spread her high heels slightly wider, locking her legs straight and arching her back. I watched her expression as my husband stepped behind her, stroking himself against her for a few seconds, then pushing all the way in, gripping the outside of her hips tight as he started the rhythm of fucking. Her eyes fell shut, her mouth dropped open, and a breathy moan escaped her lips each time his hips drove in to smack against her ass. Her eyes opened when she felt my fingers slip into her hair and pull down on her head, pressing her lips against me. She never broke eye contact as she began driving her tongue into my pussy and flicking it up over my clit, her body being pulsed forward with each thrust from my husband behind her. The three of us became lost in this moment of pleasure, each of us moaning and enjoying the other. Alison's cries begin intensifying and I could tell she was close to having an orgasm. When she finally succumbed to my husband's pounding from behind, her body shuddered and she cried out as I held her head tight between my legs, grinding myself against her lips. The scene was so erotic and with the expert stimulation from her tongue, I soon followed with a second orgasm of my own.

Still riding the waves of her orgasm, she lunged forward, climbing up my body and laying down on top of me, pressing her lips to mine and leaving my husband standing, swinging in the breeze at the bottom of the bed. It was a beautiful moment embracing her, our naked bodies intertwined and both still shuddering from our orgasms. As the waves of pleasure subsided, she broke from our kiss and smiled at me, whispering, "Let's finish him now. Remember how I made you take Robert when he came?"

With a little smile on my lips, I nodded "yes".

She smiled back and said, "Do that to me—he'll love it."

We both climbed off the bed and walked around to my husband. Both of us took him by a hand and moved him over to the middle of the floor in an open area. Pressing our naked bodies against him from each side, we ran our hands up and down his back, squeezing his ass and taking turns stroking him as we kissed his neck, cheeks, and lips. I spoke up and asked him, "Are you ready to cum for us?"

With a euphoric smile, he could only nod his head "yes".

Together, Alison and I lowered ourselves to our knees in front of him, taking turns stroking and sucking him deep into our mouths. As Alison bobbed in and out on his hard cock, I looked up and told him, "Tell me when you're ready."

After a few more minutes of us worshiping him from our knees, he began to breathe heavier and then with a rasp said, "I'm gonna cum!"

I quickly pulled him from my mouth, keeping my fingers wrapped tight around the base of his shaft, I shot my free hand into Alison's hair at the back of her head and pushed her onto him. I could see from the expression on my husband's face how intense the entire scene was to him as I pumped the base of his shaft. Watching his mouth drop open and let out a loud growl, I felt his shaft pulsing in my hand as he released deep into Alison's throat. She obediently took everything he had as I watched his body jerking with pleasure with every pulse. As he finished cumming, I pushed myself up to my feet and ran my fingers up into the back of his hair, pulling his head down to kiss him deeply and share that moment. As we passionately kissed, probing each other's mouth with our tongues, Alison continued to gently suck him in and out of her mouth as she slipped her free hand up between my thighs, her fingers sliding under to the crack of my ass, her thumb pressing in against my clit and making small gentle circles.

It was so incredibly erotic and intimate as she stimulated both of us, our lips locked with subtle moans and sighs occasionally escaping. We finally broke our kiss and looked down at Alison, smiling and watching as my husband's softening penis slipped from her lips. Helping her up to her feet, we each embraced and shared another kiss.

My husband excused himself to the restroom and left Alison and I to talk. As soon as the bathroom door clicked shut, I looked at her shaking my head in disbelief and saying "My God, that was incredible! You were amazing!"

Alison smiled and responded, "It wasn't just me—you were amazing, too."

She then added, "And I'm pretty sure he liked it," with a laugh.

"Uhhhh, yeah ... I think so too."

I just smiled at her and gave her another hug. Just then the bathroom door opened, and my husband walked out. Alison looked him up and down with a smile, then looked back at me and teased, "Think he's ready for round two?"

My husband got a nervous smile on his face and raised his eyebrows as if to ask if she was serious. She was.

I looked back at her with a smile and said, "He may need a few minutes, but I'm sure he'll be up to the task."

Once again, I took him by the hand and led him over to the bed, directing him to lay on his back in the middle. I crawled up beside him and snuggled in against him, feeling our naked bodies pressed against each other, just intending to let him rest for a few minutes. Alison walked to the bottom of the bed and stood there for a moment, just smiling and looking at us, but then slowly crawled up, pushing my top leg to the side, she laid on her stomach and lowered her lips once again between my legs, placing gentle kisses over my soft shaved lips. As she continued to caress me with her mouth, she slid her right hand up the inside of my husband's thigh and gently closed her fingers around his relaxed member, massaging and stroking it against his leg. I turned my head to face my husband, bringing my lips to his for a soft loving kiss, then asking quietly, "Is this everything you fantasized it could be?"

"Oh God, it's way better than I ever imagined—thank you," he replied in a low whisper.

Placing another sensual kiss on his lips, I then told him, "I wanted to do something really special for you—give you something out of your fantasies."

He just smiled at me and replied, "Well, you most definitely nailed it. I hope you enjoyed it too."

Just then, my mouth dropped open, and my eyes fell shut as I let out a moan when I felt Alison gently slip two of her fingers inside of me as she flicked her tongue up and down over my clit. Taking a breath and opening my eyes, I answered my husband, "Yeah, I'm enjoying it too."

My husband was amused and smiling at my response when I watched his mouth drop open and an expression of pleasure overtake his face. Alison was still slowly sliding her fingers in and out of me, but she moved her mouth over to take him between her lips and gently suck him back to life. I watched her for a moment working him in and out of her mouth, slowly resuscitating his erection.

Just then, for whatever reason, a desire came over me to make my husband pleasure her.

I got their attention and then said, "Why don't you two switch places ..."

Moving to the side, my husband slid to the bottom of the bed and Alison crawled up to lay beside me on her back. Rolling into her, I began tracing my fingertips around her breasts and teasing her nipples as I watched her push her legs open, allowing my husband to lay down between her thighs and press his lips against her. My husband was no slouch when it came to pleasing a woman with his tongue, and soon she was breathing heavily and letting out whimpers of pleasure. I alternated between kissing her lips and teasing her nipples with my tongue and teeth, my husband and I working together to send her over the edge. Her body was starting to squirm against mine and her breathing and moaning said she was close to an orgasm.

I looked down at my husband with an intense stare and instructed him, "When she cums, get between her legs and slide into her—fuck her hard."

I could tell my husband was in a place as he eagerly nodded "yes" to me while keeping his mouth pressed against her.

Returning my lips to her right nipple, I firmly teased it with my teeth as I moved my thumb and forefinger to the left and pinched and rolled it just as hard. Alison began to cry out and arch her back as her orgasm rippled through her body. As she squirmed against us, jerking and convulsing with intense waves of pleasure, my husband moved up as I instructed him, his erection now fully engorged, he drove it into her, clenching her thin hips in his strong hands. Another loud cry escaped her throat, exhaling all the air in her lungs as he began thrusting his hips against her, jerking her near limp body to him with his arms.

My husband had fucked me this way many times, but it was so erotic to see it from this angle, see how intensely hard he rammed. I knew what she was feeling, experiencing, the fullness and intense stimulation of his penetration while still coming down from her oral orgasm.

There was an odd erotic feeling overtaking me, a smile on my face as I watched her endure the intense waves of pleasure overtaking her body and knowing I helped orchestrate that.

Her orgasm subsided and her body laid relaxed, moving forward and backward, soft grunts escaping her throat with each of his strokes as my husband slid in and out of her, now at a more relaxed rhythm.

My hands were slowly caressing her breasts, but my eyes were locked with my husband's. His left hand had moved from gripping her hip and was cupping between my thighs, stroking his two middle fingers deep into me with the same rhythm as his hips. He may have been fucking her, but he was making love to me. I could see the intensity building in his expression, working himself to his own orgasm. I too was in an intense erotic place. When I knew he was getting close, I bent at the waist, sliding my head down her stomach and resting it just over her hips. With it turned slightly up, my husband was looking down into my eyes as I licked my lips and then opened my mouth, without words telling him that's where I wanted him. This imagery was more than enough to put him over the edge as he gave a final few hard thrusts into her before pulling out and slipping smoothly between my lips. In one swift motion, his hand moved to the back of my head and held me firmly as he drove himself all the way into the back of my throat and began to release. Despite nearly gagging myself on him, my right hand moved up to clench his tight ass in my fingers and pull his hips into my face as hard as I could, showing him my desire to take him. He moaned out loud as his hips twitched and his member throbbed deep in my mouth, his fingers between my legs driving deep and curling with all the strength in his forearm. He was so deep I barely could even taste him and frantically swallowed, trying to keep up with his release. After several seconds of him intensely holding my head on him, he relaxed, and I felt his fingers slip from my hair. Moving my head back, my lips gliding down the length of his shaft, I sucked gently as they left the tip, not wanting to miss a single drop of him.

Pulling back and catching my breath, I straightened my body back up beside Alison as my husband lowered himself forward, laying himself down between us. None of us spoke as we all lay there, naked and intertwined. Sexually exhausted and coming down from our alcohol, we all quickly fell asleep.

When I woke up, I was a little disoriented before everything flashed back from the prior evening. A little smile formed on my lips as I remembered the incredible experience we shared. I looked over to see my husband on his back, snoring loudly and then leaned up to realize Alison was gone.

Confessions of a Saleswoman

I pushed myself up out of bed, thinking she was in the bathroom or maybe in the kitchen, but I couldn't find her anywhere. I then noticed a note on the table outside the bedroom.

I'm sorry I had to run off, I had an early flight to catch this morning. Thank you both so much for sharing your evening with me... it was amazing!

This room is comped, so you are welcome to stay as long as you like, even the rest of your time on vacation.

Perhaps we'll see each other again, take care,

Love Alison

XOXO

CHAPTER TWENTY-SEVEN

Final Confession

After that night with Alison, my relationship with my husband was never quite the same. We are so much closer—and I could feel from him how much he appreciated that I loved him enough to create that night and explore his fantasy with him. I'll just let him think that it was all for him, even though it was partially driven by my own selfish desires as well.

I've stayed in touch with Alison, messaging from time to time online, but no plans have been made to meet again, at least not yet.

I do have many more stories from throughout the years, more confessions to share, but these were by far the three most memorable I've ever experienced. I have so enjoyed reliving these memories and sharing them with you—I truly hope you found them as arousing and exciting as I did.

PLEASE SHARE YOUR THOUGHTS

If this collection of erotic confessions ignited your imagination and left you wanting more, I would be incredibly grateful if you shared your thoughts with a rating or review. Your feedback not only helps others discover these stories but also supports the passion and creativity behind them. A few words from you can make a world of difference. Thank you for being a part of this journey!

OTHER TITLES AVAILABLE

Desiring more stories written by Sara Shae Bowman? Here are a few titles also available on Amazon and other online retailers.

- ❖ **Erotic Exposure**: A Collection of Stories About Accidental Exposure, Wardrobe Malfunctions, Getting Caught, and More!

- ❖ **Hockey Mom**: Preseason

- ❖ **Re-Do 1**: The App and I Freed to Explore

- ❖ **Tempted and Taken**: Tales of Passion, Pleasure, and Surrender

www.SaraShaeBowman.com

ABOUT THE AUTHOR

Sara Shae Bowman has long desired to share her intimate style of storytelling with the world and now is pursuing that dream. Growing up in the rural Northeastern US, the second youngest of four with two older brothers and a younger sister, Sara has always enjoyed writing, and fantasizing—and writing about her fantasies.

Still working as an attractive professional in a male dominated environment, most of the encounters in her stories are situations she has heard of, witnessed, fantasized, or even at times experienced. With millions of copies just waiting to be sold, her erotic stories are sure to titillate and stiffen your desire to read more about the professional women she lives vicariously through.

www.ingramcontent.com/pod-product-compliance
Lightning Source LLC
Chambersburg PA
CBHW020550120726
47903CB00001B/204